Sam had had rough assignments before. But never had the entire world depended on his staying alive.

Somebody with a secret formula for poisoning the whole earth was blackmailing the world's mightiest countries.

It was a secret that couldn't be kept secret for long. Sam had to find the formula before it leaked out — and destroyed all life on earth.

# ASSIGNMENT—AMAZON QUEEN

## Edward S. Aarons

A FAWCETT GOLD MEDAL BOOK

Fawcett Publications, Inc., Greenwich, Conn.

ASSIGNMENT—AMAZON QUEEN

# ASSIGNMENT—
# AMAZON QUEEN

11389

**FOR CLIFF**
**The Best of Old Friends**

# Chapter One

DURELL spoke above the thump, bang, and creak of the massive rocker-arm high above him on the riverboat's Texas deck. "Remember, there are families aboard, women and children, chickens, goats, the engine gang, maybe some river police. We don't want a panic or trouble with the locals. So you each know what to do."

"Yes," Wells nodded.

"I don't think we can do this quietly," Belmont said.

"I don't like it," Agosto said quietly.

Durell turned to the Portuguese. "What don't you like about it, Agosto?"

"He knows we are aboard, senhor. He is waiting for us to move against him. He will be ready. If anything should go wrong—"

"Nothing will go wrong."

"But if it does, we have no place to go except into the river. We are all, as you Americans say, in the same boat together. The river is wide and deep. We call it *O Rio Mar*. The River Sea. I do not swim too well, and I would not like to offer a leg or an arm to the *piraiba,* the great catfish that can eat children. The river is full of wonders, senhor, and many of them are horrible."

Durell said quietly, "Agosto, just make sure they are bottled up in their staterooms while I get the key from the girl. Then join me topside in the pilot's cabin."

Willie Wells' teeth shone big and white when a grin touched his dark brown face. There were lumps of muscle tension along his jaw. "You always get the best jobs, Cajun. But she's a wildcat."

"This is business," Durell said.

"She's had an eye on you since we left Belém."

Durell smiled briefly. "Her name is Inocenza—but she's

9

not so innocent." He looked at the dim glow of his watch dial. "We're all in synch. We'll go now."

"One moment." Agosto's soft voice interrupted. He was a Brazilian of Portuguese descent, a *moreno* whose touch of Tapajos Indian blood gave his face a flush like a burning coal, resembling the red wood known as *pau brasil*. His ancestors might have been among the Portuguese *bandeirantes* who pushed furiously into Brazil's vast interior in a hunt for slaves and loot, for plunder and glory. He was a short man, wearing a wide-brimmed straw planter's hat and a white drip-dry shirt with very long pointed collars, open at the thick, muscular column of his neck. His slacks were striped, white and black. He affected glove-leather shoes. His shoulder muscles bulged and strained against the fabric of his shirt. He was a thief, a professional, one of the best of men, so K Section's Central had reported. Agosto said, "We do not land, Senhor Sam, at Paramaguito for two hours yet. Let me try the safe myself, first. You know I am an expert at it."

"And if you're caught?"

"I am never caught yet, Senhor Sam. If so, I can handle *o capitão*."

"Captain O'Hara is tougher than you think."

"I can compete with him. He is an old man, anyway." Agosto stared at Durell. "Perhaps you do not trust me alone with the contents of the safe? I understand the big money is involved, but—"

"I don't trust anyone in this business," Durell said flatly. "The key is easier. We'll do it my way."

They were eight days out of Belém, and time was running short. The river showed no sign of narrowing. It was tremendous, awesome, a massive, mighty, incredible flow of stained water that had already coursed down for almost four thousand miles from the Peruvian Andes. Far, far off to starboard, there were a few twinkling lights ashore, four miles away. To port there was nothing but the inky, star-pricked, hot and shimmering darkness of a humid equatorial night, a sense of timeless and infinite expanse, of unthinkable power. The Amazon's volume equaled that of the next eight largest rivers in the world. It had been rightly termed *O Rio Mar,* the River Sea, by the first Portuguese explorers who had come here four hundred years ago. Ilha de Marajó was far behind them, with its countless webs of channels and seaborne traffic of rusty freighters, tankers, fishing boats, river transports, patrol launches, tugs, barges, and Indian canoes. The *Two Brothers, O Duos Irmãos,* floundered, thumped, and thrashed with its two side-wheel paddles against the full flood of the Amazon, which implacably thrust against the current on its way to the Atlantic.

"We'll start now," Durell said, "if there are no more objections."

Belmont said, "I'd like to kill that man. Andy was a friend of mine."

"Killing Stepanic won't bring Andy Weyer back to us. We need Stepanic, anyway, for another day. Or at least until we leave Paramaguito. And we don't know what consortium is backing him."

"He deserves to die," Belmont said. He was a lean shadow, a faceless silhouette, in the darkness under the overhang of the old steamboat's hurricane deck. He wore a dark turtleneck sweater, although the night was suffocatingly hot. Dark slacks and black crepe-soled shoes made him almost invisible. Durell had picked him up on the flight from Geneva to Rome, coming in from Budapest. There was a streak of white hair above his cadaverous face. He spoke Brazilian Portuguese, among other languages, without a flaw, and he had once been a member of K Section's "Q Squad," which meant that he knew everything there was to be known about killing. Tony Belmont cracked long, knobby knuckles. There was a sense of tightly leashed violence in him. The light, popping sounds of his knuckles were all but drowned in the chug, splash, and thump of the paddlewheeler's ancient engines. He said, "All right, Sam. We do it your way. But before we get the next directive, Stepanic is dead."

"I want to know who the Albanian is working for, before you do anything, Tony."

"He gets paid by the Black House," Belmont said. He almost spit the words. "Who else?"

"Then it's an off-color, unauthorized mission for him. Peking's sent an official team, a legitimate crew, on this same job."

"How do you know that?"

Durell did not answer Belmont's question.

"Let's go," he said.

He went down the ladder, a tall man with heavy shoulders, black hair streaked with gray at the temples, eyes that were dark blue, sometimes black when he was angry or thoughtful. For his size, he moved with a lithe grace and a balanced silence. He had worn a moustache until some years ago, when it became an identifying item in his dossier in Peking and in the files of the Foreign Directorate of the Soviet Committee of State Security—the *Komitet Gosudarstvennei Bezopastnosti*—the KGB. Then he had shaved it off, but his survival factor according to the computers was still dangerously low, and he had been granted, without asking for it, a bonus in his annual contract with K Section, that troubleshooting arm of the Central Intelligence Agency run by General Dickinson McFee. He had made a habit of caution until it was primal second nature, an instinct imprinted on all the nerve-patterns of his neural and muscular system. He was careful opening doors, turning corners, entering any room, however familiar the setting might be.

Durell knew the dirty nooks and crannies of the world's jungles and great metropolitan centers intimately; he spoke a dozen languages fluently, along with a score of minor dialects. If Tony Belmont was an expert at killing methods, Durell was Belmont's tutor. Durell could kill or maim in any number of swift, silent ways. He did not like to. It was sloppy, it left ripples in his wake, and he preferred to move about unnoticed and unremarked, and, particularly, unidentified for what he was by local police. He thought he might have to put some extra restraints on Belmont, although Tony was not like that madman he'd been forced to work with in Malta. Unlike Keefe that time, Belmont had brains. Which might just make him more troublesome than Keefe had been, on this strange job.

He regretted the death of Andy Weyer. It was Andy's fault, of course. Andy had been careless in Belém; he was supposed to stay at Durell's side, helping to guard what Durell carried with him. Perhaps Andy had been overanxious, and impatient with the blackout in which the whole team had moved for almost two weeks now. But in Durell's business, you could not look back for too long. Andy Weyer and Belmont had been partners for some years. It was a tough break. Stepanic had proved smarter than Andy, and you paid dearly in this business for one moment's hesitation, a split-second decision that might prove wrong. You died silently, almost carelessly, without oratory or accolades, and always officially by accident. Belmont was wrong to feel personally involved in Weyer's ugly death. Emotion had no place in the business. It could kill you.

Still, it was a good team, patient under the lack of information they all possessed, not knowing where they were going, or why, in this strange paper chase. It was like being a pawn in a child's game, except that they operated in deadly seriousness, moving so far around the world, from Washington to Geneva, from Addis Ababa to Tokyo and then to Belém and then aboard the rickety-rackety chuffing *O Duos Irmãos* going upriver on the immense Amazon to a destination none of them could even guess at.

Durell had decided tonight not to follow orders blindly any more. He had come far enough. It made him uneasy not to be in command of the situation.

At the foot of the ladder he paused, oppressed once again, since boarding the old side-wheeler, with a heavy wave of nostalgia, of *déjà vu*, of having been here before. For all practical purposes, the overcrowded riverboat was not new to him. He knew every inch of each deck, every companionway, stateroom, gallery, cargo holds and the engine room of the *Two Brothers*. He could have made his way blindfolded about the ancient, shuddering vessel, and never err.

Long ago, as a boy, he had been brought up on this vessel's sister-ship, the *Trois Belles,* beached in the mud of Bayou Peche Rouge in Louisiana, after a long life as a gambling paddlewheeler on the Mississippi. He had lived alone there with his grandpa Jonathan until he went off to Yale for a law degree and then, by one step and another, had entered the employ of K Section, under that remarkable little gray man, General Dickinson McFee. As a young boy in the bayous, Durell had been taught to hunt, and had learned the tricks of the hunted, too, in the dark green abysses of the delta country. He knew the ways of wild things as well as he knew the evasions and wiles of men. His years aboard the *Three Sisters* with old Jonathan, while the riverboat moldered in the muddy dock in the bayous, had taught him all there was to know about the gallant breed of riverboats that had once breasted the currents of the Mississippi channels. It was like coming home again, to be aboard this throbbing, chugging, reeking old vessel that nosed through the channels of the mighty Amazon.

Someone came down the ladder after him.

He paused at the rail, not turning his head. He knew it was Willie Wells by the light, springy footsteps.

"Cajun?"

"Take it easy, Willie. You belong up forward."

"I'm on my way. I was wondering—"

"Yes?"

"You know the skipper of this stinking hulk?"

"He was a friend of my grandfather's."

"You sure of that?"

Durell turned. "Why do you ask?"

"Why did Cap'n O'Hara leave the Mississippi?"

"He was bought, along with this boat, maybe seventy years ago. O'Hara was just a young man, then. He'd been mate aboard the old *Trois Belles* once, my grandfather said. He mentioned O'Hara once or twice."

"Good or bad?" Wells asked.

Durell looked at the wide, enormous river under the vibrating black tropical sky. There was no relief from the heat, even by the movement of their passage. A barge and tug lights moved against the darkness, perhaps two miles away.

"Not very good," Durell admitted.

"Your Grandpa Jonathan didn't like O'Hara?"

"I think not. He didn't talk much about him. It was a long time ago, Willie."

"But you remember it, don't you?" Wells persisted.

"Yes, I remember it. A Brazilian rubber baron, during the wild rich days of the rubber boom up here on the Amazon, wanted a riverboat and bought the *Two Brothers,* lock, stock, and barrel, had it dismantled, crated, and shipped to Manaus, where it was reassembled, renamed *O Duos Irmãos,* and was used as a private yacht in Senhor Claudio Villas Jeronymo de Sousa's service."

"You been doing some homework, Sam?"

"I just happen to remember it." Durell paused. "But it was a long time ago, Willie. Those frontier days on the Amazon are gone forever. The rubber boom ended and the rubber barons moved out. But O'Hara somehow kept this steamboat. That's all there is to it."

Willie Wells stood almost as tall as Durell, a lithe strong man with the air of a predator about him. Maybe all the men in K Section's Q Squad looked this way, Durell thought. Wells, after a bitter tour in Vietnam, had been a black mercenary in Africa when Durell first met him. Willie called himself a citizen of the world, and his reaction to Brazil—where all men were color-blind and saw only the man, not the color of his skin—was strange. Wells was affronted. His fierce pride in his black skin made him want to be recognized for what he was. He had been estranged from society through an ugly childhood in the ghettos of Philadelphia. Later, when Durell helped him get a contract to work for K Section, the man proved to be ruthless, dedicated to whatever employer paid him for what had to be done. His devotion to a job was implacable. Once, in Ceylon, due to a misunderstanding of orders, Wells had even set out to kill him, wiping from his mind the fact that Durell had been his benefactor. Durell had beaten him that time, but he would never look forward to a second encounter.

He saw Wells' white teeth flash in his black face. "Is something bothering you, Sam?"

"A little. It's of no importance."

"Something about O'Hara?"

Durell said, "We're on a paper chase, Willie, as I said. We don't know what our orders will be in Paramaguito, right? Maybe we'll be sent off in another direction."

"Yuh. A strange job, this one is."

"But an important one."

Wells hesitated. "You're carrying a lot of money on you, Cajun."

"So is our competition."

"Do you know who they are, yet?"

"Some of them. They're coming from everywhere, all over the world. Maybe they're being summoned, like us, by different routes. But we know Stepanic, anyway. Get on forward. Time is running out."

Wells grinned. "Good luck with *a pobrezinha*—the poor little girl." He chuckled. "Inocenza. What a name. No noise on that one, huh?"

"No killing," Durell said. "Only to save your own life."

## 2

He waited until Wells vanished along the broad curve of the hurricane deck, then went down one more ladder and moved silently forward. The paddlewheeler turned slightly to port, following the channel buoys in the maze of the enormous river. The swinging bow revealed, far, far ahead, a dim pinpoint of light from the river port of Paramaguito. It would be just about dawn when they docked. He looked at his watch. Behind him, the massive sidepaddles churned and splashed. The steamboat shuddered through a dark tangle of driftwood floating down the current from hundreds or thousands of miles upstream.

She was waiting for him in the warm, private darkness of her special cabin.

The riverboat was crowded with transients, travelers to

the interior, farmers, Indians, road-builders, the flotsam and jetsam that collected along the watery highway, including those who couldn't afford or couldn't find available air transportation. Aboard the *Duos Irmãos* were shoestring traders, unemployed, vagabonds, men, women and children, all those whose business had taken them from one infinitesimal spot on this gigantic river to another. He was acutely aware of the press of humanity packed aboard, of the sounds they made in their sleep, of a single dim light in one cabin where men in stained whites gambled with greasy cards, while tethered chickens huddled in a corner of the stateroom. He heard the bleat of a goat somewhere aft, where Stepanic had managed a suite of rooms along with his assassins.

He tapped lightly on Inocenza O'Hara's stateroom door, tapped again, then tried the lever handle. It opened easily. He felt better. She had expected him.

"Sam?"

Her voice was a whisper, intriguingly accented.

"Yo."

"Oh, I have been waiting. I think you never come."

"Well, I'm here," he said.

"Lock the door, please."

"Yes."

"And draw the curtains."

He did as her voice requested. A dim, rosy lamp bloomed in the darkness. Her breath came in lightly, expectantly. She was O'Hara's adopted daughter, but where he had ever picked her up, or why, he hadn't learned yet. But he meant to. She was as unlike the gross, gray-grizzled old steamboat *capitão* as a jungle orchid is to slops thrown to swine. She had turned up in Belém as his contact when he was directed to take passage aboard *O Duos Irmãos*. She'd been all business then, quick and direct, wearing a lightweight, fashionable suit, dark sunglasses, looking as much a part of the smart Brazilian scene as the most social of its esteemed society. Something had passed between them, however, in that brief, businesslike meeting. When she took off the opulent sunglasses, her eyes were the palest of blues against the darkness of her suntanned Latin face—a face as pure-looking in its oval perfection as a saint's. Inocenza, she called herself, and smiled. But the eyes gave her away then, as they did now.

"You like me, Sam?"

"I like."

"You thought of how I would look, naked?"

"From the first moment," he said.

"As I did, with you. We understood each other, eh?"

"Yes."

"So I have been waiting here."

"All night?"

"Since we left Belém. Come here, Sam."

Her slender body, with proud breasts and womanly hips, moved; and when she moved, on the wide, plush ornate bed that had somehow been installed in this miserable hulk of a riverboat, the golden chain around her neck swung a bit, from nipple to nipple, revealing the crucifix and the key to the riverboat's heavy, improbable safe.

She laughed, a throaty sound. "Come, Sam. You never saw a true *Amazona*? In the olden days, when people believed such women as I were warriors, it was true, in a way. I shall do battle to you, in this bed."

"Inocenza—"

"Please. Come here."

She pushed her hands up behind her neck, turning her lustrous, heavy black hair into a waterfall. He shook his head, smiled, and checked the cabin in the rosy light of the bedside lamp. There were heavy red velvet curtains over the two cabin windows, but they did not reach to the deck. No one could be hiding behind them. The bed was very high, with enough clearance for a man to squirm under it. There were two doors, darkly paneled, with brass locks and polished knobs. Hanging in gimbals were two brass and glass globe lamps, Victorian in style, perhaps part of the riverboat's original equipment. He moved to the doors on either side of the bed and tested them. They were solidly locked. Inocenza, crouched on the bed, made a pouting expression with her ripe mouth.

"What is it, Sam?"

He smiled. "I don't want to be interrupted."

"One of the doors is to my bathroom. It has a big old-fashioned tub that stands on gilded lion's paws. It is all my own. The door on the right opens to a ladder going up to the wheelhouse, where I sometimes stand watch, and O'Hara's quarters. Sam, darling, I've been waiting almost too long."

He sat down on the bed beside her. He had his gun, a .38 Smith & Wesson Special, tucked into the waistband of his slacks. She saw it, looked up at his face, and began to unbutton his shirt.

"You are a strange man, Sam Durrell. You come to me armed with such a weapon. It is not what I wanted to see. Are you some kind of policeman? Or a bandit? Do you and your friends plan to hold up the boat?"

"Nothing like that," he said. "Inocenza—"

She had his shirt off. Her breasts pushed against his chest. The nipples were hard, eager. Her dark hair hung in a screen across her face. Her ripe mouth smiled.

"No talk now, Sam. Hurry."

He felt a vibration underfoot as the paddlewheeler again changed course. "Where did you get the bruise?" he asked.

"Oh." She touched the side of her forehead with quick, startled fingers. "It still shows?"

"How did it happen? An accident?"

She shook her head. "No accident. It was O'Hara."

"Your stepfather hit you?"

"He often does. But this was the last time. The next time, I put a knife in him. Or slice off his *homem*. I told him so. I promised it to him—a slice where he will never molest a girl again with his dirty tricks." She looked suddenly vicious. "He has treated me like a slave of the old days, all my life, since I was of twelve years. He bought me from some people upriver—yes, bought me, such things still happen up there. I do not know why he wanted me, until two years later, when he forced me. I was truly innocent then. Later, after it went on for a time, I made him stop. I threatened him with the knife. But the beatings went on, when he taught me about the river and the boat. Last week will be the last time, I said."

"Why did he beat you last week?"

She looked away. "It was nothing."

"Why?" he insisted. "Was it in Belém?"

"*Sim.* Yes."

"While you were waiting for me to come aboard?"

"It had nothing to do with you. It was Manoel."

"The first mate?"

"Manoel loves me. He wants to marry me. He wants to live on the river and have a steamboat for himself. I hate it. I hate the river. I will not let him have me." She wriggled on the bed. The gold chain swung, snuggled between her proud breasts. "I am famished for you, Sam. Please."

The boat was silent except for the endless thump and clank of the rocker arm high above that drove the big, splashing paddlewheels. In the ruddy glow of her glass bedside lamp, Inocenza looked infinitely appealing, ultimately lovely. He felt a pang of regret at what he had to do.

He held her breast, touched the chain and the key and the golden crucifix there. The metal felt warm in his fingers. She fell forward against him, crouching. Her mouth was warm and hungry. She made words with her lips against his.

"Always it was *Capitão* O'Hara. Oh, how I hated that fat, ugly old man! He couldn't—" She touched him. "He was not like you. He needed—I cannot say it—he was not young and smooth and hard like you, Sam. So long I dreamed of one like you, one I could truly love, who would take me from this terrible old boat, from that terrible old man—"

"Inocenza, no."

"No, what?" she laughed in her throat. "You say no with your lips, but not with—not with this—"

"I want the key to the ship's safe," he said bluntly. "I need it. Right now. Later, I'll try to come back."

She drew back as if he had struck her. Her face showed rage, chagrin, and then a kind of animal cunning. She touched the chain between her breasts. "The key? At once? Is that why—"

"I'll be back."

"Then you *are* a thief?"

"Not exactly."

"You come here to use me, just to get the *key*?"

"Inocenza—"

Her abrupt fury was that of the Amazon jungle, her speed that of a jaguar. Her claws scratched for his face as she lunged forward. He did not want to hurt her. Given time, he could have removed the key from her neck-chain without her knowing it. But there was no time. He could not make love to her, whatever she thought. He tried to evade her long nails, caught her wrists, forced her hands down. She fell on top of him, her body hot, writhing, smooth and supple. She was stronger than he had suspected. Her breath hissed as she sucked in air to scream. He did not want to hit her. But there was no help for it.

He tried to measure the strength of the blow, but it was not quite enough to knock her out. She fell sidewise from the bed, hit the floor with a thump on her naked buttocks. Her grip dragged him down on top of her. Instantly her legs scissored, holding him to her.

"Inocenza, give me the key!"

"I shall call for Manoel. For O'Hara," she gasped. "You know what they will do to you? You know how it will look, you break into my cabin, you attack me?" She began to laugh under his weight. "Later, I may give you the key. It depends all on you. If you please me. If you make good love to me."

He hit her again, harder.

This time her eyes rolled and her smooth, struggling body went limp under him. He waited a second or two, to make sure she was not feigning. Her mouth was open; her white teeth glinted between her lips. There was a small trickle of blood from the corner of her mouth, where his knuckle had cut her slightly. He lifted himself, yanked the gold chain from around her neck, took the key, and stood up. The girl did not move. He was not particularly pleased with what he had done.

## 3

Agosto, Tony Belmont, and Wells were waiting in the deep shadows of the deck behind the square pilothouse atop the Texas deck of the paddlewheeler. Their faces looked pale in the dim glow reflected from the steamboat's riding lights. Behind them, the great iron rocker arm lifted and fell like some strangely jointed, antediluvian river monster, the *screak* and thump of its power covering any sounds they made. It was significant that none of them asked about the girl when he appeared. Durell preferred to work alone, under normal circumstances; but this was hardly the usual task he was assigned to perform; and the three men were competent, tough, and dedicated to the business.

Agosto held a dead chicken by its legs. Its neck was broken. On the narrow deck behind the pilothouse, a man in white trousers and cotton jacket lay face down, his arms sprawled.

Wells said, "The guy was chasing his chicken. It got loose and came up here. Belmont hit him."

"Dead?"

"Not quite."

Belmont said, "He was in the way."

"All right," Durrell told him. "What about Stepanic?"

"There is one main door leading to his suite. He could get out a window, I guess, after he discovered the door is locked and barred. He's in there with his people."

"Did they hear you?"

"I doubt it. No alarm."

Durell nodded. "In we go."

"Are we taking over the boat?" Belmont asked.

"Later. Not right now."

He went in first, sliding around the corner of the pilot house to the narrow door opening from the deck. Only a dim binnacle light shone inside. The figure of the young first mate, Manoel, was at the big wheel, conning the steamboat into the channel toward the distant glow of Paramaguito. The door was locked. Durell rapped softly on the yellowed glass. The pilot turned his head, shook it, and looked away. Durell rapped again, making the sound insistent. The pilot's good-looking young Indian face became annoyed. At the third rap, he lashed the wheel with a wide leather thong and came across the pilot room to unlock the door.

"It is forbidden for passengers—"

Durell moved in fast, knocking him aside. Belmont followed, slamming the muzzle of his gun into Manoel's throat. Wells and Agosto followed softly. The little cabin was crowded. The deck trembled underfoot. From far astern, down below, a woman called a man's name in a worried voice.

"It's the chicken fellow's wife, I think," Belmont said.

Durell returned to Manoel. "We want to look into your safe. We do not want the ship's money. Just a look at what Captain O'Hara has in there."

"I do not have the key, senhor." Manoel's voice was tight and hard with anger. "You have no right to do this to me. We will go aground." He spoke in a lilting but gutteral Portuguese. "You must let me go back to the wheel, senhor!"

Wells said, "Let him, Sam. I don't like the thought of going into this river with all those piranhas—"

"No piranhas here," Agosto said, "but let him take the wheel, *sim*? It would be best."

Durell nodded. "Let him go, Belmont. You'll break his larynx. But if he yells, hit him."

Manoel's eyes flashed with sullen anger. He understood English. "*O Capitão* O'Hara will have you skinned alive for this. Are you bandits? We carry no gold, no gems, no cash, no payrolls for the road workers. Only poor river people and their chickens. You are not Brazilian police. You are not bandits or terrorists. Then why do you do this?"

"Just steer the boat," Durell said, "and you won't be hurt. We only want to look into the safe."

"It holds nothing of value to you!"

"I'll decide that. Didn't Senhor Stepanic leave some paper with you?"

"Only a thin envelope. A nothing. No money in it, senhor!"

"He didn't take it out of the safe, did he?"

"Senhor, he said he would take his envelope when we dock at Paramaguito. In an hour, perhaps. At dawn. He will leave the ship then—he and his Chinese friends."

Durell turned to the rear of the cabin. There was another narrow, varnished door, and this led him into a tiny room filled with charts, empty liquor bottles, a flat mahogany table scarred by knives and by the rings left by countless liquor glasses. In one corner stood the safe. It loomed massive and heavy in the dim light. He stuck his head out the door for a moment.

"Willie? Agosto? Out on deck. Keep watch. Belmont? Control the pilot."

"No sweat," said Belmont.

"Don't hurt him," Durell said.

He went back to the safe and took the key he had lifted from Inocenza O'Hara. The safe was a huge iron Schmidt-Alexander, and it probably dated back three-quarters of a century, perhaps to the time when the steamboat still worked up and down the Mississippi. It had been built in Cincinnati. The ornate gold lettering on the door had been touched up once or twice, and the dark green paint was worn around the old combination dial. The dial didn't work. It had been replaced by the key lock drilled into the iron door, and he put the key in quickly, thinking of the dawn coming up soon astern. He was filled with a sense of urgency, of impending danger far beyond his personal safety or that of anyone on the riverboat. He had felt from the start that he was only one fly among many, caught in a dark spider's web, following his own strand, while others, like Guerlan Stepanic, followed theirs. The trail to this point had been long and puzzling. Perhaps, he thought, they were not like flies, but mice being trained to follow a maze carefully, with bait at the end of the trail. He did not know their ultimate destination. His orders from Washington had been precise, but they had placed an intolerable burden on him. Other men, following their alleys in the maze, had an equal burden. Each was an enemy, a rival, determined to outwit, to out-think, and, if possible, to destroy the others and arrive alone at the end of the maze. Someone was playing a desperate game with them all, and Durell had decided to end his role as a willing victim and strike out for himself.

He shook the thoughts from his mind. He had to take one step at a time.

Inocenza's key fitted smoothly into the lock of the massive old safe. There was a soft click as the tumblers fell aside. He pulled the handle on the door decorated with faded gilt curlicues and dulled enamel paint. There was only a dim light in the chart room. The interior of the safe was like a black hole. Most of the compartments were empty. There were two bottles of J&B Scotch, some Olmeida Portuguese brandy, a heavy old Colt's Frontiersman that looked as if it were part of a hand-fashioned pair. On a shelf in the rear of the safe was a brown tin box with a flat key in it. He opened it quickly, saw it was filled with wads of both new and old cruzeiros, the former worth one thousand of the old bills since the currency reform in 1968. He didn't touch the money. He closed the box, left the key in it, and searched further. There was a pile of old, mildewed papers, some of them the ships' licenses and certificates going back for thirty years. He sifted through them impatiently, then in the middle of the heap, found the new manila envelope he was looking for.

Written on the face of the envelope was *Senhor Guerlan Stepanic,* Paramaguito, Brazil. Under the envelope was another, marked with his own name: *Senhor S. Durell.* And a third that stopped him, frozen with surprise. *Prince T. Atimboku.*

Durell swore softly. He opened Stepanic's envelope with a quick, slashing movement of his fingers and turned back to the light.

The certificate was not there.

It should have been a money note, an irrevocable letter of credit drawn on a Swiss bank, with the recipient's name left blank. It should have been valued at anywhere from fifty million dollars on up.

It was not there.

He was not too surprised. His own envelope was also empty, as he had arranged it to be. Guerlan Stepanic would not have truly trusted the safe, either.

He had no time to look farther.

There was a thump on the deck outside the pilot house. Another thump, a scuffle, a dragging of feet. Footsteps sounded in the pilot room adjacent to the safe. Durell's face went blank. He tossed the envelope and papers quickly back into the safe, closed the door, started to withdraw the key.

A rusty, grating voice that sounded as if its owner hadn't been sober in a decade spoke behind him.

"Hold it just like that. One move, and I'll be happy to blow your goddam head off. Keep your hands at your sides, huh? Now turn around, real slow like."

He did as he was ordered. He told himself it was impossible, with three good, efficient agents to hold back anyone who might interrupt him.

But it had happened.

He stared at Captain Jack O'Hara.

The man's gross, bearded bulk seemed to fill entirely the narrow door to this little room behind the wheelhouse. He wore striped pajama pants and scruffy leather bedroom slippers, and above the top of his pants his huge belly bulged like a small beer keg, and his heavy chest glinted with a mat of sweaty silver hair. There was black hair in thick pads on his pale, suety shoulders, contrasting again with the baldness of his scalp and the silver-white of his unkempt beard. An odor came from him, a mixture of sweat, garlic, and stale whiskey. But there was nothing careless in his narrow, pouched gray eyes and nothing uncertain in the way he handled the big mate to the pearl-handled Colt's Frontiersman .48 that Durell had seen inside the safe. The muzzle looked as big as a yawning tunnel mouth, drilling steadily into the middle of Durell's stomach.

Durell spoke quietly. "How did you do it, Uncle Jack?"

"I ain't your uncle, sonny. You got a gun on you? Course you do. Keep it where it is, hey? Who told you to call me 'Uncle'?"

"My grandpa Jonathan. Jonathan Durell. He owned the *Trois Belles*. Still lives on it. He spoke of you now and then."

The gray eyes grew as cold as death. "Yeah? Good or bad?"

"Neither. He just mentioned you, from the old days on the Mississippi. It was a long time ago, when I was boy."

"You got a good memory. Old Jonathan, hey? I thought he was long buried, the bastard."

"He's alive. In Bayou Peche Rouge."

"He would be. Yup, I knew the old son of a bitch. We was friends, once. Long, long time ago. I forget. That's why you bothered me, sonny. You look a little like he used to be. Your ma and pa still livin'?"

"No. They died a long time ago."

"How?"

"An auto accident. How did you get the drop on me?"

"And your grandma?" Something flickered in O'Hara's wet eyes. "She was a lovely gal. Clarissa?"

"She's dead. She died quite young. After that, Grandpa Jonathan beached the steamboat and never sailed her again."

"I see." The fat old man grinned and dropped the past. "I got a pad on the roof of this here pilothouse. Nights like this, on the river, I sleep up there. That Inocenza pesters and pesters too much. A man my age likes to sleep alone, once in a while." O'Hara's grin was as evil as the breath of hell. "You got to her, hey? Little tramp. Tried to raise her decent. But you got her key, I see."

"I stole it," Durell said.

"Don't try to cover for her, Samuel. You ain't all as smart as you think you are. I'm getting paid good for what I'm doing, and I don't aim to lose the balance of the cash that's promised me. I can move real quiet. You wouldn't think so, would you? I heard you and your men pick off that caterwaulin' Manoel, at the wheel. He's lovesick. Dreamin' of Inocenza's tits, most likely. So I slipped down real easy and came up behind your man outside. That's Agosto, right? Jazzed him right into the cabin with my gun up his ass and made the others, your other two boys, keep real quiet. Gave Manoel a gun to hold on 'em and walked in on you. What you doin', robbing my ship's safe?"

"I wanted to see what Senhor Stepanic had in there," Durell said mildly.

"Why?"

"We're business rivals," Durell said.

"What kind of business?"

"Uncle Jack, you talk too much."

The old man grinned. "A failin' of mine, picked up from these Brazilians. Been on the river too long, maybe. But if you don't answer, Samuel, I think I'll blow a hole right in your gut. Right now."

He meant it.

# Chapter Two

IT HAD begun over two weeks ago, in Washington, D.C.

"Take the skipjack," McFee had said. "Norman Apple will go with you. He's with the DIA now. Defense Intelligence is in it, too. You know Apple, don't you?"

"Yes, sir," Durell had said.

"You don't like him?"

"I didn't say that, sir."

"You won't have to work with him. Just sail the boat down to George's Fields. You know the point there?"

"Yes, sir."

"Just take a look at it. This afternoon. It's a nice day for sailing. We don't know who might be on surveillance down there, and this has to be kept to ourself, between us and Sugar Cube. The White House gave us specific orders on that. So play it innocently. Look and report."

"What do I look for?" Durell had asked.

"You won't miss it. It will be big enough."

Durell paused. "I haven't renewed my annual contract, sir. I'm not sure I will, after what happened in Ceylon."

"I wish you would forget all that," McFee told him. He brushed the air with the back of his small hand. "You still have two weeks before the contract runs out. Perhaps I can manage a bonus. You're living in Deirdre Padgett's house for the time being, aren't you?"

"Yes. She's in Rome again."

"Miss her?"

"Yes, sir. Like my right arm."

"I'll have her back for you when this is finished."

"Is that a bribe, sir?"

"Of course," McFee admitted. His gray eyes permitted a little amusement to show. "Mr. Apple is waiting for you at Prince John. At Deirdre's house. In an hour."

"Yes, sir."

Norman Apple was a ruddy-faced, ebullient man who knew nothing about sailing. He was no help with the skipjack. The converted Chesapeake Bay oyster boat leaped before the early spring wind, her huge sail bellying like a white wing. Apple considered the day's outing as a holiday. He wore a striped singlet and electric-blue belled stretch slacks, and had had the sense to change into sneakers. His face was open and candid, belying somewhat a keen intelligence and a high capacity for efficient action. His straw hair blew in the wind over the Chesapeake, and he fumbled happily with the lines of the skipjack under Durell's commands. The sun was warm, the water sparkled, and the low slopes of the Eastern Shore loomed green and inviting, with stretches of sandy beach, an occasional crowded marina, a chugging tug hauling a stream of barges upstream to Baltimore.

"You have any idea what this is all about, Cajun?"

"We'll see for ourselves," Durell said.

"I wish I could have brought a gal or two along. This is great. Why didn't I ever take up sailing before?"

Durell considered McFee's brief words. It was not often that he could detect tension in the little gray man. He thought he had sensed something in General Dickinson McFee's manner that wasn't quite normal. McFee was not an easy man to work for, and Durell had learned from several difficult experiences that nothing superseded the success of an assignment, neither life nor death or personal attachments, in McFee's mind.

The skipjack heeled in the freshening breeze. A tanker came downstream from Annapolis. Durell stood with an easy balance at the wheel. He had worked hundreds of hours refurbishing the old vessel, scraping paint, replacing rigging, remodeling the oyster boat's hull into spacious, comfortable cabins below. He eyed the puffy white spring clouds, noted the chop of a cross-current as he watched the shore. Speedboats raised white plumes on the western side of the Bay, along a series of marshes that were havens for duck hunters during the season. The sun had laid a beneficient hand over the fields, woodlands, and small white towns along the shore. He filled his lungs with the salt air. He watched a school of fish splash, and considered the bounty of nature, the softness of the sky, the inestimable wealth of growing things—

Until he rounded the skipjack toward the Eastern Shore and spotted the Coast Guard patrol vessel, apparently on routine duty, three miles from George's Fields.

"Get the glasses, Norm," he said quietly.

"Are we there already?"

"In a few minutes."

"What are those buoys for?"

"It's apparently a restricted area," Durell said.

"Something new?"

"Yes."

A series of blasts from the patrol boat's horn warned them off. Durell obediently turned the wheel over and headed farther offshore. Slowly, as in a turning diorama, the area of George's Fields came into sight, dimly at this distance.

The change was abrupt and shocking.

"Got the camera, Norm?"

"Right here."

"We'll need the new GX5 telescopic lenses."

"They're classified, Sam."

"So are you. You were directed to bring them, weren't you?"

"Yes, but we're not authorized—"

"Do as I tell you." Despite himself, Durell caught a harsh note in his voice. Something prickled on the back of his neck. "Start taking high-intensity pictures, please."

"What's wrong over there on shore?" Norman Apple's voice had changed, too. The DIA man's freckles stood out against a sudden pallor in his skin. "Oh, Jesus, what's happened to that place?"

"McFee will tell us. I think he just sent us out here like this to impress us."

"I'm impressed," Apple whispered. "Also, I don't mind admitting, more than a little scared."

George's Fields formed an outward bulge in the shoreline, and normally the ten-square-mile area was a center for fruit growers, orchards, tidy white houses, and the neat little village center on the shore, with its pilings and docks and small boatyard doubling the productivity of some of the richest farmland in the area. Durell held the wheel steady with his thigh and took the glasses from Apple. The scene leaped into quick, sharp focus. It was as if a line had been drawn across the neck of the point, separating it from the main body of the land beyond.

To the north and south of George's Fields, the farms and trees were lush with new spring growth, blowing in the light warm wind that came from the southwest across the Bay. Through the glasses, Durell could see that the main road turned off the highway into George's Fields, and the police kept a roadblock there. Two other feeder roads were similarly blocked, and with the help of the lenses, he saw a number of men moving slowly along on foot patrol, cordoning off the entire point of land. All of the men were heavily armed. Some were in uniform, but most of them wore civilian clothes as they probed cautiously along on the green side of the barrier.

Nothing grew on the other side, in George's Fields.

Nothing moved.

There were no blossoms on the fruit trees.

There was no sign of life in the small village that nestled in its cove beside the blue shore of the Chesapeake.

There were no new leaves on the trees.

Everything was brown, desolate, shriveling, dying.

"How—how many people in George's Fields, Sam?" Apple whispered.

"About five hundred, I believe."

"Are they all dead?"

"I think they must have been evacuated. But maybe they're dead, yes." He scanned the area further from the deck of the heeling skipjack. The wheel pushed anxiously against his thigh as the spring wind freshened. "No, there are some cattle. No calves, though. Some horses over there, near a paddock fence. No foals. It's as if—"

"Oh, Jesus," Apple said again.

"Yes. The whole area has been sterilized."

"Sam—"

"I don't know why or how," Durell said.

"You think it might have been an accident—with one of our own devices?"

"Sugar Cube ordered a ban on all CBW warfare material. Most of the stockpiles, maybe all, have long been disposed of in the Atlantic. No chemical, biological, bacterial warfare equipment has been permitted, by directives from the White House."

Apple whispered again, "But maybe an accident—"

"I don't think so."

"It hasn't been in the press, on the radio, or on TV. Where are all the George's Fields *people* being held?"

"McFee will tell us."

"But if it wasn't an accident, due to our own stuff—"

"That's right."

"—then it was a—a sort of sample of something from someone, somebody else."

"A demonstration," Durell said. "A threat." He told Apple to take more pictures while he took a long last look at the desolate fields, the trees that bore no blossoms, the grass that had not seeded itself. Inwardly, he suddenly shivered. It was something new. Not immediate death to living things. Perhaps something far worse. No growth, no calves, no foals, no fruit. And no babies born. His voice was hoarse as he said, "Are you finished, Norm?"

"We don't need the pictures," Apple said. His words were peculiarly flat. "Nobody could forget this, anyway. And besides, we seem to have enough people in charge over there on the land. I feel sick. Could I be seasick, Cajun?"

"No."

Durell turned the bow of the skipjack into the wind, let the sail flap, then turned on a direct tack back across the Chesapeake toward Prince John, on the green, living shore opposite.

A small plane droned by, high overhead in the pale, springtime sky. It followed their same course.

## 2

Deirdre Padgett's house in Prince John was an old rose-brick Colonial set back on a wide lawn from the shore, under big old elms, oaks and sycamore trees. There was a small landing and a gray boatshed down by the water, and a brick path led up to the inviting white doorway. Durell had been living here for the past two weeks, while Deirdre was in Europe. He'd been waiting for his new contract and a new assignment. The place was home to him, the only true home he'd ever known since his youth in the bayous aboard the hulk of the old *Trois Belles,* with his grandpa Jonathan. But anywhere with Deirdre was home, he told himself. There was a serenity about the gentle house that echoed the peace and love he had found in Deirdre. He had a momentary ache for her, wishing for a glimpse of her dark coppery hair, her oval face, her soft mouth and quiet voice, her rich woman's body that he knew so well. The ache for her became a sudden pain, echoing the memory of what he had just seen. He kept his face impassive as he tied up the skipjack to the little dock. From behind the boatshed, he heard Norman Apple vomiting.

Three men in dark suits, white shirts, and dark neckties, with shoes polished to a high gloss that reflected the sunlight, came down the walk from Deirdre's house. One of them Durell recognized as Homer Carboyd, one of the President's most confidential advisers. He was a stocky, barrel-shaped man with florid face and a thick shock of pure white hair. His angry blue eyes were set deep under heavy, bristly brows.

The second man was from State, Kevin Kendall, one of those rare, dedicated, intelligent men whose blunt brilliance kept him from the upper echelons of the bureaucracy, but whose incisive mind was always respected, despite the sneers of those diplomats who deplored Kevin's lack of Ivy League background.

The third man was General Dickinson McFee, whose small stature was deceptive. There was an aura about

McFee that made him seem bigger than his companions. He was all in gray, as usual, and he swung his blackthorn walking stick with no trace of impatience. That stick, Durell knew, was loaded with every lethal protective and agressive personal gadget that the lab boys could devise in the basement of K Section's headquarters at No. 20 Annapolis Street. It made Durell a bit nervous when McFee pointed the stick at him.

"Ah, Samuel. Did you have a good look?"

"Yes, sir."

"Where is Apple?"

"He'll be along in a minute."

"Yes. I hear him. Well, there's no time for delay. We've set things up in the living room."

"What things, sir?" Durell asked.

Homer Carboyd made a grumbling sound. "Let me brief him, Dickinson."

Durell looked at Kevin Kendall, whose fifty-odd years looked fortyish. Kendall smiled faintly. His dark brown eyes measured Durell like a camera, weighing, judging, deciding him, all in one swift, comprehensive glance. His melodious voice still held a trace of Boston Irish—another feature that his more elegant coworkers at State often deplored.

"You understood what you saw at George's Fields?" Kendall asked.

"Part of it, Mr. Kendall."

"Good. General McFee places great faith in you— much more than anyone at Sugar Cube, Treasury or State. I think McFee is correct in his analysis. Sugar Cube considered sending an army, virtually. McFee insists that one man, or a small team of men, would do. Come along, Mr. Durell."

Durell paused. "An army?"

"Overreaction. It's a violent world." Kevin Kendall waved a blunt, disparaging hand. "I spoke figuratively."

Two long black limousines were parked on the shell driveway in front of the columned entrance to Deirdre's pink-brick house. The town of Prince John, a mile away, slumbered in the warm sunlight. A cardinal screeched in a budding maple tree. Squirrels chattered at him. Norman Apple, appearing with a pale face and mumbling apologies, was delegated to watch the two official cars.

A chart on a tripod, covered with a sheet of blue cloth, had been set up on the old oriental rug in the living room. The three men had made themselves at home in Deirdre's place. They had helped themselves to drinks from the bar, moved the shining Chippendale table into the area of the bow window that looked out on the clipped lawn and the little beach and the bright expanse of the Bay. The smell of cigar smoke from Homer Carboyd's eternal stogie—actually, a Havana cigar imported from a London tobacconist, much to the President's private annoyance—clung heavily to the light, figured draperies. Durell felt a brief touch of resentment at the way these men had intruded themselves into this quiet, calm house where he and Deirdre had spent so many highly personal and intimate days together.

As if aware of his thoughts, McFee said, "I spoke to Deirdre in Rome, Samuel, asking her permission. She sends you her love and tells you to be careful."

"I think I should be, in this company." Durell smiled. The other men were too grim, he thought. Too nervous. Their tension made the atmosphere crackle. It was as if they had replaced all the glory of the growing springtime outside with a darkness, a gloom that held in its dark cupped hands an omen and a foreboding.

"Samuel?" McFee said quietly.

"Yes, sir."

"Before we discuss the problem of George's Fields with you, you must agree to accept the assignment. I admit this is a bit unusual and irregular. But the problem we have here is under the direct supervision of Sugar Cube." McFee nodded slightly to the stocky Homer Carboyd. "If you do not accept these terms here and now, we must place you in temporary confinement until the matter is resolved."

"Arrest me?" Durell said. "On what grounds?"

"Call it national security," Carboyd grunted. "Are you going to quibble about it? McFee says you aren't that kind.

I'm not so sure." Carboyd swung heavily to McFee. "I'm not sure at all but what the President isn't right about all this. It's not a job for one man or half a dozen men. We need every possible agency on the job. And we need a man we can trust, a man who can be counted on to insure the safety of unlimited funds." Carboyd glared at Durell. "I mean that literally. Unlimited funds."

Kendall said in his gentle Boston voice. "The instructions are clear, Homer. No more than half a dozen men." He turned his slender body to Durell. "Mr. Carboyd is talking about a truly unlimited amount of money. Hundreds of millions. Perhaps more. And your ability to stay alive. And at the end, to trade accurately, shrewdly, perhaps ruthlessly, for what has been offered to us."

"Tell me what it's all about," Durell said flatly. He sensed tension and danger in the room, directly not merely against himself, but against the whole nation. Perhaps the world. "Tell me, and then I'll decide whether to do it or go into custody."

"Quite sensible," Kendall said blandly.

Homer Carboyd relit his Cuban cigar. "All right," he snapped between his teeth. "Show him."

McFee walked to the chart on its stand and lifted the blue cloth that hid its surface. It was a map of the world. It did not seem particularly significant. Then he crossed the living room and scanned it more closely. He stared at it for only a moment; but everything imprinted on the chart would stay in his memory.

He touched a point on the map. "Is that George's Fields?"

"Yuh," Carboyd said. "You want a drink, Durell?"

"Not yet."

"Pour him one, Kendall. He'll need it."

Durell touched another point on the map. "And this, in the Soviet Union?"

Carboyd said, "A collective farm, *Drashnaya Kolvetzniya*. Fifty miles from the Kremlin. The other red dots—the one in Red China, for example, is a commune about forty kilometers from Peking, one of their showcase combination farm and industrial-factory units. Shantze, I think it's named. You'll note other places, one in just about every large nation of the world. Plenty in Western Europe —England, West Germany, France. One in Israel, a kibbutz not far from Tel Aviv-Yafo. One in Egypt, too. A couple in Africa—the one in Pakuru, for instance. McFee tells me you did a nice job there, not long ago."

"The niceness depends on your viewpoint. Prince Tim Atimboku was and still is a son of a bitch," Durell said. "I assume that all these places are in the same condition as George's Fields?"

"You assume correctly."

"And they all went sour simultaneously?"

"Just about."

"Is it a plague?"

"No."

"A biological warfare mishap?"

"No. You know it couldn't be. Not in all those places at once."

"Has George's Fields been analyzed?" Durell asked.

"The works. We've given the people there biological, physiological, X-ray, EKG, blood tests, sera—everything. There are no results except that the women haven't ovulated and the specimens of semen from the mature males are all negative." Carboyd's voice rasped. "We have biologists checking the plant and animal life in the whole area. For the time being, we've put the inhabitants of George's Fields incommunicado—a camp out West. So far, we've kept it from the press. But that can't succeed forever."

"When did this first begin?"

"It was noticed ten days ago."

"Did anything happen then?"

"No one heard, felt, or saw anything."

"No trucks in the area, spraying the trees?"

"The orchards were all sprayed by normal means, regular contracts. We've checked it all out. We thought that might be how it was done, sure, but a spray wouldn't account for the animals and the people. We're checking the tanks, the trucks, the drivers. Everything negative, so far."

Durell said, "Did any planes go over, at that time?"

"A few. Some light private planes. The usual jets from

Washington to New York. We've covered the airports, big and small, everything from Kennedy to every pasture-type landing field for hundreds of miles. Every flight seems normal, those we've been able to check."

"One of them couldn't have been normal. If it wasn't done with spray trucks, it had to be a plane. Here and abroad." Durell paused. The three men watched him. He met their stares with an impassive stare. "You're holding something back?"

"It's foolish." Carboyd coughed and glared at Kendall. "About ten days ago, one light plane in the night circled George's Fields several times, as if it was in trouble. At least, that's what Old Annie said."

"Old Annie?"

"Mrs. Annie V. Carruthers. She's ninety-six. The George's Fields people think she's a witch. Or screwy. Always claimed she could talk to the animals, the bees, the birds."

Durell said, "We should check her hearing."

"We have."

"And?"

"She has an extraordinary range for high notes." Carboyd walked to the Chippendale table and picked up several folders of massed documents, waggled them in his pawlike hand. "These are all affidavits and statements from the people who lived in George's Fields. They are all within normal parameters except for old Annie's. She says she heard, or felt, the vibrations of the wings of the Angel of Death."

There was a pause. Durell said, "Was this the night the light plane circled over the area?"

"We don't know. As I said, there are planes going over every night. We've put NASA's big computer to work, figuring permutations and combinations. If Old Annie actually heard or sensed stress vibrations that no one else got that night—"

"Vibrations," Durell said. "Cell-crushing sounds too high to be detected, destroying only selected items such as reproductive cells in plants, animals, and men?"

"We have chemists and biologists and whatnot on it.

The consensus is that it's all impossible. It's being worked on. The Russians, Chinese, French—you name it—are all working on it, too. The upshot is zero, so far. But we've only just begun." Carboyd chewed angrily on his cigar. It had gone out again. His broad face looked redder than ever. McFee sat down, considering his heavy blackthorn stick as if he had never seen it before. Kevin Kendall looked quietly out the window. Carboyd said, "We're all up against it. I personally don't believe it. George's Fields is there, granted, but it's a hoax. Nobody would have the consummate gall—"

*"Chutzpah,"* Kendall said deliberately.

"Don't give me your Yiddish idioms," Carboyd said angrily. "Why do you like to denigrate yourself, Kevin?"

"It's a perfectly good word to express what you are trying to say, Homer."

Carboyd ran fingers through his shock of thick white hair. "Do you see any humor in the problem, sir?"

"If it's a hoax, as you suggest, it's funny in a rather grim, frightening way," Kendall said gently. "We live in a world of terror and violence. Our streets, our planes, our public meetings are targets for confused, anarchic men who use our modern technology to terrorize, assassinate, and gain ransoms for themselves or their causes. Now we're up against what may be an ultimate bluff. The entire world is at stake—the future of all life, making us the last generation on earth, if we are to believe the ultimatum we and all the other nations involved have recently received."

"Do you believe it's an ultimatum or a hoax?" Carboyd snapped.

Kendall said quietly, "George's Fields, and what happened to every living thing in that area, is only too real. So we have to pay the piper, for all our mistakes in the past." Kendall lifted an eyebrow to Durell. "We've tentatively labeled the thing the Zero Formula. Zero, for all future life on earth. You have to find it and buy it for us."

"On one condition," Durell said.

"Yes?"

Carboyd started to say something in heat, and Durell added, "My condition is that the thing be destroyed. At once, without fail, without hesitation, equivocation, or compromise."

Kevin Kendall nodded. "Sugar Cube wants it that way, too."

# Chapter Three

THERE WERE techniques laid down for everything in K Section's procedures, Durell thought—even to having an ancient .48 Colt's Frontiersman rammed into your belly by an outrageous, fat, bearded old river rat who made a living on a rattletrap side-wheeler on the Amazon. You learned the procedures on the Maryland "Farm" and then you relearned them again, and yet again, every time you came home for rest, recreation, and reassignment.

It was suddenly very hot in the crowded pilot house of the *Duos Irmãos*. It smelled of sweat and anger and fear. What had started back at George's Fields on the Chesapeake was not going to end like this, Durell thought. He felt the steamy dawn wind off the vast river blowing through the slanted windows in front of the big polished wheel. He caught Wells' eyes. The black man smiled and blinked twice.

A strange look had come over Captain O'Hara's red face. Even the bristles of his unkempt beard seemed to quiver with hatred. It went beyond a normal outrage against Durell for prying into his ship's safe. There was something personal in it, something vindictive, as if the fat man longed to pull the trigger of his revolver and send every bullet smashing into Durell's body. Something else touched the man's pale, rheumy eyes, and Durell recognized it as a flicker of fear, wonderment, puzzlement. But mostly fear. It seemed exaggerated for the situation.

"Why?" O'Hara grated. "Why'd they send *you,* Samuel?"

"Why not?" Durell spoke carefully against the man's explosive fear and anger. "It's my job, O'Hara."

"But why *you?*"

"I don't know. Should it have any significance?"

"You're lying!" O'Hara shouted. He stepped back a bit in the crowded pilothouse. His slippered feet made no sound on the deck. His small eyes darted to Wells and the solemn Belmont and the swarthy-skinned, calm Agosto. He shook his head like a battered water buffalo. "No. They—he couldn't know you'd have to come on my boat. No. He couldn't guess it. Samuel, when you started out, did you know you were coming here?"

"No."

"But it couldn't be an accident." A dribble of saliva appeared in the corner of O'Hara's mouth. His huge chest heaved as he breathed in gustily. The stink of stale beer and garlic was on his breath. "It's been a long time since I seen the Mississippi—seen your old grandpa Jonathan and his woman—"

"My grandmother," Durell corrected quietly.

"Right. A smart, pretty woman, she was. But—"

Wells made his move. Manoel at the wheel had glanced down briefly at the vessel's compass and then out forward at the closing lights of Paramaguito. Wells' move was a lethal black fluidity, a strike so quick it fooled the eye. There was dull sound of flesh against bone as the black man hit Manoel in the nape of the neck. As the ship's mate slumped, eyes rolling, Wells caught the gun from the Brazilian's hand. O'Hara made the mistake of letting his eyes flicker at the brief noise. Durell chopped down at the fat man's gun with his left and drove his right fist low into the man's vast belly. It was like hitting the solidity of an unripe pumpkin. The man was tougher than he looked. The air went out of O'Hara with a low grunt and he tried to bring up his big Colt again, and Durell hit him with two fingers in the throat, chopped at the side of his neck with his left, and O'Hara slammed back against the wheel. It should have knocked him cold; but it didn't. The man stared, his chest heaving, his eyes slitted with bright pain. Durell scooped up the big gun and held it pointed at the fat captain. Wells came around to steady the wheel, and O'Hara suddenly kicked at him—and Wells' gun went off.

The report was like a vast explosion in the pre-dawn

quiet of the paddlewheeler. One of the panes of glass in the pilothouse shattered.

"Hold it," Durell snapped to Wells.

Over the endless thump and clatter of the engine and paddlewheels, he heard a woman suddenly scream, astern in the crowded cabins. A man shouted dimly. Durell gestured to Manoel's body. "Did you kill him, Willie?"

"No." Wells looked disgusted. "The fat pig almost surprised me, though."

"Wake Manoel up. We'll need him. O'Hara?"

The steamboat *capitão* grunted, ran fingers like sausages through his grubby beard, rubbed the back of his neck where Durell had chopped him. His pale eyes were malevolent. "Jonathan sent you, after all these years, huh?"

"No. Not my grandfather. Let's have the next set of instructions, O'Hara. The ones in your safe. Mine and Mr. Stepanic's."

"I can't do that. I sure can't—"

"Hurry it up." Durell's voice was suddenly harsh with implied violence. "The ship is waking up. Belmont?"

The cadaverous man hadn't moved through it all. His eyes were amused. He looked chilled in his black turtleneck sweater, despite the humid heat. In his dark slacks and black crepe-soled shoes, Belmont was like a waiting shadow, always timing himself for the right move.

"Whatever you say, Cajun," he murmured.

O'Hara blustered. "They're in with my charts. Over there. But you won't make nothin' out of it. It's just orders for your next move, see? For Stepanic, too."

"Who hired you, Captain?" Durell asked.

"I can't tell you that. I don't know. You think I'm afraid you might kill me? That's nothing. I'm an old man. Forget it, don't ask me, because you'll never learn anything from me."

Agosto said quietly, "There are ways, senhor."

"You ain't got the time, sonny. We're landing in half an hour."

"And if we stop the boat?" Durell suggested. "We can wait in the channel until your tongue loosens up, O'Hara."

The fat man chuckled. Suddenly he was affability itself. "And have a riot aboard? You don't know the kind of crazy peons we're carrying. They'd get scared and drop chicken shit all over the place. They'd riot, tear the boat apart, afraid we were sinking or something."

"Someone paid you to hold the instructions for us at Paramaguito. Who was it? A local man?"

"I wouldn't know. I received the envelopes, I got five thousand new cruzeiros, and I accepted the job, no questions asked. I don't see five thousand every day."

"He's lying," Agosto said calmly. "He is the first messenger we have been able to get our hands on, Senhor Cajun. The very first, at all the places we had to stop to get here. Always the messages were telephoned, or waiting for us. He knows what we must know."

But what O'Hara said about the steamboat was true. The vessel was overcrowded, and the sound of the shot that had aroused the first woman had now caused a growing hubbub all through the ancient boat. It was like a swelling tide of terror, a growing clamour of shouts, crashes, women's screams, mingled with the contagious bleating of goats, the cackle of chickens, the barking of dogs. If they halted the boat now, the panic would rise to bedlam.

Belmont came back from the chart rack with two manila envelopes. Durell snapped open the one with his name typed on it.

> My dear Mr. Durell and your colleagues—
> Your aides are really not necessary for the success of your mission. But you will proceed to the Hotel O Rei Filipe in Paramaguito. Please leave luggage and equipment aboard the vessel. Further instructions will follow. Obey Capitão O'Hara. I trust you have brought enough money. The bidding will be high. I assure you.
>
>                               S.

Durell folded the envelope in his pocket and opened the instructions for Stepanic. The wording was identical. He scanned it twice, could detect no difference. The message was written on an old Portuguese typewriter with accent marks accompanying the letter type in odd places. The paper was a fine linen weave, tinted pale blue. It smelled slightly of mildew. When he sniffed it, he caught Wells' eye on him.

"What now?"

"We'll do as it says."

"Anything about the money?"

"Whoever 'S' is, he's anxious that we have enough."

"I don't like it," Wells said. "He keeps us all in the dark. We don't know where we're heading."

Durell looked at Captain O'Hara, who had found a brown cigarette butt beside the wheel, and seemed only concerned with lighting it without setting his beard on fire.

"Who is this 'S'?" he asked quietly.

"I sure as hell don't know."

"You read these messages, didn't you?"

"They were sealed, weren't they? How could I? I ain't interested, anyway. I got paid to do a job, to deliver you to wherever you was told, and that's it." O'Hara cocked his bald head to one side. "I think we're gettin' company here."

There were shouted questions from the deck below the pilothouse as a surge of passengers headed for the ladder. Durell nodded to Belmont to take over and stepped out through the narrow varnished door. There was a pearly radiance in the east, heralding the new dawn. A heavy mist clung to the vast reaches of the river. The air felt warm and wet. The big iron rocker arm that drove the splashing paddlewheelers groaned and clanked overhead. From the twin stacks came belches of foul-smelling black smoke, visible now against the lighter sky. Two Indian crewmen came up the rear ladder to the Texas deck and hesitated, talking to each other excitedly. They pointed, not at Durell, but to something or someone on the other side of the pilothouse. Durell moved around there fast—and slammed into Mr. Guerlan Stepanic.

Durell was lucky. The Albanian was not alone. There were two Chinese, tall Manchurians in dark Western clothes, behind Stepanic. Durell's gun covered them before any could move. Stepanic sighed and spoke in a bored way to the two flat-faced Chinese.

"This is unfortunate. Let it not be said that we acted in foolish haste, Po. The gentleman is Samuel Durell, the American imperialist spy, agent for capitalistic colonialism."

"The same old clichés, Stepanic?" Durell asked. "Are your friends hatchetmen from the Black House?"

"Really, now." Stepanic's English was flawless, touched with a British public school accent. He was a lean man who might have passed for the most genteel of diplomats, with his sleek hair and hawk's face, his elegant gray moustache, his immaculate grooming even here, on the Amazon, aboard a wheezing, rattletrap riverboat. But Guerlan Stepanic was head of the *Gotosji,* the assassination section of the Albanian intelligence command. "Really," Stepanic drawled, "did you think to steal my directives from poor O'Hara's safe? You've aroused the whole vessel to a tumult. Most clumsy of you, my dear Cajun."

Durell did not lower his guard. Inside the pilot house, he could see Manoel at the wheel, conning the ship toward the channel to the dimming lights of Paramaguito. The sky was brighter, promising the sharp, sudden tropical dawn on the Amazon, although the mists on the river persisted. The air smelled of mud and decayed debris floating down from the countless tributaries of *O Rio Mar.*

Stepanic said easily, "You went to much trouble to steal my instructions. Most unethical of you, Mr. Durell. However, no matter. I already know them."

"You are not an authorized emissary to the auction," Durell said flatly. "Peking has a committee of its own, on the way. You're working for a rogue branch of the Black House. I trust you realize that. As a consequence, you're beyond the rules of this game."

"Rules? There are no rules in this affair or any other that concern us, my dear Cajun. The only precept to follow is to win."

"Did you kill Andy Weyer, in Belém?"

"Tut-tut. You can prove nothing."

There was a clamor on the ladders to the Texas deck. A flood of passengers, some in pajamas, some in the ubiquitous white jacket and ragged pants, straw hats, and naked feet, poured over the rail, yelling for the captain. The panic had spread from the single gunshot. Men, women, and children suddenly crowded and pushed around the pilot house, undeterred by the angry shoves and shouts of the few crewmen who showed up.

"Best put away your gun, Cajun," Stepanic repeated softly, "or these poor, ignorant peasants may mob you. Come, Mr. Po. You, too, Lin. We have nothing to fear."

Durell did not try to stop them as the Albanian and his two grim, silent Chinese pushed through the yelling crowd. Belmont suddenly stood beside him. The tall, thin man was shivering. "I'll get him," Belmont said. "I swear I will."

"You'll do only what I tell you," Durell said shortly.

"Is he going to the same place we're headed for?"

"Yes. Stepanic, and a lot of others. All of them out to cut each other's throats and reduce the competition—including our own. So let's be careful. Doubly careful, now." Durell looked at the loom of the approaching docks of Paramaguito. "I think we're close to the end now. And the closer we get, the tougher it will be to survive."

## Chapter Four

"Yes, it is an invitation for murder," Kendall had said. The State Department man had flown with Durell to Geneva over a week ago. Kevin Kendall was calm, in obvious control of himself. "You have heard it all, Sam. What do you think?"

"It's difficult to believe," Durell said.

"You have a tremendous responsibility. An enormous burden of trust upon your shoulders. And you will be moving into possibly the worst danger of your life."

"I don't mind that," Durell said. "I just can't figure out the ultimate purpose of the whole thing. I'm used to the danger. But I want to know this maniac's real aim."

"It's an auction," Kevin Kendall said. "An offer to sell the Zero Formula to the highest bidder. There has never been anything like it before. We are up against a most astute mind, one that cannot be underrated. Once you get the letter of credit, you are on your own. It's a laboratory maze set up for poor little mice—and you're one of the specimens, Sam."

"If I get my team, we'll have some sharp teeth."

"You will have all you need," Kendall said softly, "and my personal blessings and prayers, whatever they're worth."

There'd been no time wasted since the briefing at Prince John, on the Chesapeake. Everywhere in the world, in most of the major nations and in some of the lesser but more volatile countries, there had been an example to match what had happened at George's Fields. Two days after the demonstrations, the first messages arrived to the heads of the various states. They were ultimatums, blunt and uncompromising. The Zero Formula was briefly described as a new device designed to sterilize all growing life in any area to which it was applied. There was mockery and a deliberate vagueness in the description that set the country's top biologists, medical men, chemists, agronomists, and CBW people into a desperate, around-the-clock effort to analyze and synthesize the device. It was no use. The evidence was there, clearly demonstrated. At George's Fields, all growth had stopped. The human population was hospitalized and tested. Plant biologists had taken specimens of trees, grass, weeds, every flowering bush and shrub. All reproductive activity had stopped. The life in George's Fields continued, apparently toward its normal span. But no new generation could follow.

No one should have been surprised, Durell thought. In this world of geometric progression in technological growth, almost anything seemed possible. Kevin Kendall had put it most bluntly, when he had addressed Homer Carboyd.

"I don't care how much you bluster and fume, Homer. We have absolutely no clue to who perpetrated this act. It may be that we are dealing with a madman. If so, it is with one who has access to a number of national territories—access with a freedom to plant, sow, or irradiate specific areas for his damned demonstration. Our photo satellite CP-242 has spotted all of the affected places, as far as we can tell. We've been in touch with various heads of state. Some of them, of course, promptly denied everything. But when we admitted George's Fields, the Kremlin discussed their collective at Drashnaya Kolvetzniya. Peking allowed as how something had gone wrong with their showcase commune at Shantze. The Egyptians refused to discuss Al Gharam. The Israelis are bitter about their kibbutz at Tefanya. West Germany, England, France are amenable to open discussion. Frankly, we're all frightened. The African nation of Pakuru, headed by Prince Tim Atimboku, refused to discuss anything, promptly blaming the nation to the north to which they refer simply as the 'Neighbors.' Japan is withholding comment."

Carboyd made a grunting sound as he relit his Cuban cigar. "Damned foolery. Together, the whole world can't be hijacked!" He hesitated. "Can it?"

"Yes," Kendall said softly. "It can be. It is. Because there's no answer in sight to what has been done to George's Fields."

"The President feels that by international cooperation—a joint refusal to pay ransom, so to speak—"

"Then there will be other, bigger, worse demonstrations. Perhaps whole cities will be sterilized. Perhaps your state of Kansas, with all its wheat. Life could end, sir, in this generation."

"It's a holdup," Carboyd said angrily. "A damned game. Somebody is laughing at us, all right."

"Yes. And the terms are most peculiar." Kevin Kendall turned to Durell. "You see, the messages delivered to the world's heads of state have stipulated an auction."

Durell stared at him. "The Zero Formula is up for grabs to the highest bidder?"

"Not only that, Sam. Each nation is to send an emmissary to an as yet undesignated place, where the Zero Formula will be put up on the auction block and sold to whoever is willing to pay the highest price."

"As I said," Carboyd grated. "It's a holdup."

"What's money?" Kendall asked. "Can you compare it to the potential consequences? Can we allow anyone else to bid higher for this horror? We simply cannot allow any man to perpetrate this sort of thing on the entire world."

"It can't be one man," Durell said. "It must be an organization. The demonstrations took place simultaneously. That demands a lot of men, trained to distribute the formula. It could be the Russians, or the Chinese, covering up a hijack."

"The instructions," Kendall said, "specify that an intelligence agent be sent. The same orders went to our—ah—competitors. Israel and Egypt, being too volatile, have not been invited to the bidding. A nice touch, that. The Japanese, Swiss, the West German Bundesnachrichtendienst—the BND—have declined to participate. Sadly, some countries have decided to play it close to the vest and will not give out their intentions."

"How much is the asking price?" Durell inquired.

Kendall laughed. "The sky is the limit. It's been stipu-

lated that an unlimited credit letter on a Swiss bank, with
the payee's name left blank, be given the agent-bidder. It's
pretty foolproof. The point is, everyone will try to stop the
competition from getting in a bid. Just arriving at the auction—wherever it's to be—will take a miracle for any
man. The Soviets and the Chinese will surely send their
best people. McFee thinks you're our best choice. Think
you can do it?"

Durell said, "How much time do we have?"

"We've been given two weeks. On the 27th of the
month. But we don't know where the auction is to be, as
yet."

Durell said, "But suppose I make it? Suppose I succeed
in buying the Zero Formula and then live through the return trip. Every other agent will be after me and the formula. The top people, the best assassins. The setup shows
a rather warped mind, to devise this thing. Someone wants
to be amused, in a peculiar way. It won't be easy. But I
want to be assured about the disposition of the Zero Formula when—if I get back."

"The President will decide all that. Obviously, we all
feel it must not fall into irresponsible hands. You *must*
succeed, Sam."

"How do I get to the auction block?"

Kendall spoke quietly. "Each step of the way will be
marked by new instructions, we are told. Your first leg is
to come to Geneva with me and set up the financial arrangements. You'll be responsible for hundreds of millions
of dollars. Really, unlimited funding. At the Chantilly
Hotel, you will be told where to go next." Kendall paused.
"There are no stipulations that you proceed alone. You
can pick your own men."

Durell had thought, *Why me?*

He should have been flattered that the three most powerful men under the President had chosen him. He had
been in the business for a long time, longer than he cared
to remember. Nothing like this had ever happened before.
A collection of the world's deadliest, most efficient, most
dedicated agents were to compete with each other for a
technological freak device, a device that could be used by

any ambitious, violent nation against the rest of the world.

Several things bothered him about it. He thought it showed a macabre sense of humor. He felt as if someone was playing with him. And he was not at all sure that the end would be what Homer Carboyd, General McFee, and Kevin Kendall expected.

## 2

The Jet d'Eau sparkled and splashed in Lac Leman under the cool sun of Switzerland. From the balcony of their small suite in the Chantilly, Durell watched a lake steamer from Ouchy-Lausanne head for the docks to his right. Across the bright water, the hills and spires of the Old Town lifted against a flawless sky. The distant Alps to the south were heavy with snow.

Inside the suite, Durell had turned the radio up loud. On the balcony, Kevin Kendall shivered. His silver hair gleamed in the pale sunlight.

"It's cold out here."

"It's safest," Durell said.

"Why do you think the hotel rooms are bugged?"

"They must be. We were directed to stay here, even told what suite to take. It had been reserved for us by cable from Madrid, and prepaid." Durell had gone through the baroque rooms with the proverbial fine-tooth comb. The faded settees and cushioned chairs yielded nothing. He had turned up the carpets, taken the beds apart, checked the heavy draperies with their tarnished gilt tassels, making certain that each hanging, each picture frame was clean. It was a tedious job, but he was patient about it. It took an hour before he discovered the loose plaster angel among the others in the ceiling corners. It yielded slightly to the pressure of his finger. The others were fixed solidly. He took a chair and stood on it to reach the height of the ceiling, and then noted impressions on the carpet where someone else had placed a chair similarly. Very carefully, he moved the winged cupid, which had had its nose chipped off and regilded some time in the past. The plaster casting was hollow. Inside, he saw the bugging device, small and gleaming, a complete tape recorder that was self-contained on long-life batteries, voice-sound activated. He did not disturb it. He replaced the cupid and put the chair back where it belonged, then turned on the radio and took Kevin Kendall out on the iron-railed balcony.

"Why did you leave it there?" Kevin asked curiously.

"It can't do us harm, as long as we know about it. We might want to feedback some misleading data, too."

"Yes. Well. I am not aware of the refinements of your profession, Sam." Kevin took the envelope he had returned from the bank with. He had gone to a *privat bankier,* an unincorporated firm named Bank Bloch, which had been set up by K Section with a Swiss, a M. Bloch, as a front. Kevin's face was solemn. "You can bid up to two hundred million, to start with. More funds will be available, if necessary." The Bostonian hesitated. "It's a lot of money. A clever man, with an open letter of credit like this, working within the rules of the Swiss banking system, could dispose of these funds throughout the world and never leave a trace. You understand that, Sam?"

Durell's smile was thin. "Don't you trust me yet? Do you think I'm about to abscond with it?"

"It's a great responsibility. I don't know that I'd care to be trusted with it." Kevin shivered slightly in the cool wind that blew off Lac Leman. "I wouldn't trust myself. No man knows what he may do, under unforeseen circumstances. How will we be able to communicate with you?"

"Part of our job setup is to have Centrals all over the world," Durell said. "I have a GK-12 transceiver, as well. It's small, but powerful. It still may not carry far enough, depending on our ultimate destination, but it's the best we've got. I'll try to report regularly."

"You have only eleven days left," Kevin reminded him.

"Yes."

"You must be very careful. Where will you keep the letter of credit?"

"It will be on my person."

"Isn't that—ah—risky?"

"The whole thing is a risk. If I'm taken, or if our competitors stop me, the whole thing blows up for us, anyway. It's a race for the fittest, and our opposition will send in their best people."

"But all that money—"

Durell said drily, "Rest assured, Mr. Kendall, I'll guard it with my life."

## 3

He waited quietly through that evening, dining at the hotel, taking a split of wine from the lake vineyards. Kevin left on a 1600 Pan Am plane from Cointrin Airport at Geneva. The hotel dining room was not particularly crowded at this season of the year. The winter economy tourists had left and the summer invasion of hippies and college kids had not yet begun. There was an air of leisure and relaxation at the Chantilly.

Andy Weyer arrived first.

He had flown in from West Berlin, where he had been working with the West German BfV, the equivalent of the FBI, on internal security. Weyer looked like a youthful college professor, his light brown hair rather longish, his sneakers dirty and scuffed, his sack suit rumpled. He seemed uncomfortable in a shirt and necktie. He had an engaging smile—a smile that never touched his eyes, if you looked closely. He had been recruited by K Section during a semester's sabbatical and had given up his chair in ancient history at Wesleyan to devote all his time to the business. He took to work for the agency with a sense of relief, as if he had found his niche in life. He was a natural. He was tall, but not as tall as Durell, with a lithe body as lean as a whip. He had trained himself diligently and applied his scholar's mind to work at hand with enormous success. He wore horn-rimmed glasses, which gave him a professorial look at odds with his beard and long hair.

"Yo, Cajun."

Durell liked him. "Good to see you, Andy."

"This is a tough one, they tell me. A kind of paper chase, they said."

"Yes, that's the phrase. It's a no-limit, hands-off assignment," Durell told him. "I don't know much more about it than you, Andy. I've sent for Tony Belmont from Syria. And we'll pick up Willie Wells and Agosto, who's in Lisbon, wherever we go next. For the moment, we sit here and wait for instructions. How are you armed?"

Andy Weyer shrugged. "Knife, gun, thermite bomb, a bit of plastique. Is it in Europe?"

"We don't know where we'll go, until we're told. That will be whenever they get around to it. You're not to leave me, Andy. If I go down, you're to get the letter that's in my zippered belt. *Get* it, no matter what. Understood?"

"Yo," Weyer said. "Do I know what's in it?"

"An unlimited letter of credit on Bank Bloch, with the payee's name left blank."

Weyer laughed. He had good white teeth. He liked to eat organic food, and looked with distaste at the remains of Durell's dinner. "I'll watch you like I was glued to you, Cajun. Like we were Siamese twins, right?"

"Right on," Durell said.

They waited in the suite through the long hours of evening. Andy said, "Certain aspects of this thing get to look curiouser and curiouser, as Alice said."

"Yes."

"There has to be an organization," Weyer decided. "A very good one. Headed by a top man."

"Yes."

"I know I'm covering ground you've already considered, Cajun. Just let me consider it aloud. Whoever devised the Zero Formula is a scientist, an academic brain. That sort of mind doesn't normally go on to develop such an elaborate, whimsical scheme as this auction-to-be. We're in Alice in Wonderland, I think. Or maybe following a thread through the fabled Minotaur's labyrinth, like Theseus. We should be so lucky as Theseus was in ancient

Crete, long ago. It suggests a certain *modus operandi,* I'd say."

"I have Charley Weintraub working on the m.o.'s of every top intelligence agent for the past thirty years. No farther back. This one wouldn't be that old. It's somebody who has retired, defected, quit, or simply vanished. So I have Weintraub going through the dead files, too. The computers have not come up with anything yet."

Andy Weyer crunched raw nuts with his strong teeth. He ate them by the handful. From his baggy coat pocket, he took out a packet of raisins and began eating them, too. His eyes were thoughtful behind his horn-rimmed glasses.

"Suppose Charley doesn't find anything?"

"He must. Whoever developed the Zero Formula has a partner, an agency man like ourselves, but a top one, who knew enough to demand that only operatives of first-class stature be assigned to this auction. It's a rather macabre game," Durell said. He had ordered a bottle of bourbon from the Chantilly's bar, and he poured some deliberately, aware of Andy Weyer's disapproval. "It's somebody who knows our names, our dossiers. Not just K Section people, either. From every intelligence department in the world. Even the Shin Bet, in Israel."

"How many bidders will there be?"

"At least a dozen. Perhaps more," Durell said. "Every one an expert, every one deadly. And each of them anxious to stop any or all of the others from getting to the auction."

"And afterward?" Weyer asked mildly.

"Even if we're successful in bidding high enough to get the thing—and making certain there are no duplicates and that the inventor comes back with us—there will be the problem of getting safely back to Washington. The competition will be after us like a pack of hounds. We'll be going into a nest of snakes, Andy. There won't be any rules. No gentlemen's agreements, either, afterward."

"It's a sticky one," Weyer agreed. "Maybe I should have borrowed one of our new tanks."

**4**

The telephone rang.

The voice was a tape recording, deliberately distorted by mechanical filters so its true identity was impossible to guess. Durell thought it was a man's voice; Andy Weyer thought it to be a middle-aged woman's husky contralto.

This message will not be repeated. You are to go to Rome on Alitalia Flight 202 leaving Cointrin Airport at 0600. At the Leonardo da Vinci Airport you will go to the Antiquita Tour Agency on the upper level and receive tickets for your next destination. No more than four of you, including Mr. Durell and Mr. Weyer, will be permitted to travel farther. The schedule is tight, gentlemen. We wish you a safe journey. For the moment, you are in no danger. The other travelers who will also bid are proceeding to our mutual destination by various routes. You should not cross their paths until the end. Good luck. And take good care of the money!

Andy Weyer blew air out from between thinned lips. "They know everything. Even about me."

"Which confirms my idea," Durell said, "that there is an intelligence apparatus at work in this."

"I swear, nobody followed me from Berlin."

"They didn't have to."

"You mean there's a leak in our own group?"

"Not necessarily. Just that we're under surveillance, very good, very professional."

"Doesn't that bother you, Cajun?"

"Not yet," Durell said.

"It bothers me," Weyer said. "Like a goldfish in a bowl. We're also like monkeys on a string."

"We'll snap the string when I'm ready. Let's get some sleep."

Tony Belmont joined them in Rome, coming in from Beirut. The cadaverous man, who had continuous Q clearance, had a peculiar affinity for Andy Weyer. Belmont was older, quiet, and had on his record six official kills for K Section. He was a professional assassin whose genius was directed against enemy counteragents and double agents from Peking's Black House and twice from the KGB, his victims being men whose sole job was to disrupt, terrorize, or eliminate anyone who stood in the way of enemy expansionist and subversive policies. His attitude toward Andy was that of an older brother, quietly protective. Andy would have resented it if it had been too overt. The two men were close friends. In a sense, Durell envied them. He had never permitted himself the luxury of a close attachment that might cause hesitation at a critical moment, a delay or a shading of perspective on the job.

Their next flight was to Addis Ababa on an Air Ethiopia 707. The ticket agent at the Rome airport knew nothing about the purchaser of their tickets.

"They came yesterday, signor. Is all paid for, all reservations confirmed."

"Where did they come from?" Durell asked the man.

"Please. I know nothing. It is not my purpose to question such things, is it? They came by mail, cash included."

"What kind of cash?"

"Italian lire, sir."

"Do you have the envelope the tickets came in?"

The Italian spread his hands regretfully. "I am sorry, signor. It was thrown out."

"Do you remember the postmark?"

"Ah. Of course! An Ethiopian airmail stamp. My son collects stamps, sir. I saved it only, not the envelope. They came from your friend who waits for you in Addis Ababa."


On the flight over the Mediterranean, Belmont said quietly, "I've been thinking of Delacroix, Sam."

"The artist?" Weyer asked.

"No. You wouldn't remember this one, in the business. He was in the Resistance Movement in France, during the Nazi occupation. A Belgian, really. He ended up as a colonel in NATO intelligence, and about five years ago he just dropped out of sight."

Durell said, "He ran the Nazis on a paper-chase scheme, too. Swiped some of their loot, led them from one clue to another, and in the end, booby-trapped and killed them." Durell paused. "But Delacroix is dead. He was killed in the Congo, where he'd gone to retire."

Belmont nodded. "What about Mansciewicz? Polish. He liked elaborate schemes, too. I remember a game he played on the Russians, three years ago, when there was a worker's strike and a local uprising—"

"They shot him for it," Durell said.

Belmont's cadaverous face was calm. "Do you have any prospects in mind, Cajun?"

"Three. A monster named Dr. Mouquerana Sinn, first. I ran into him in Sri Lanka—Ceylon—not long ago. He took over Madame Hung's private intelligence apparatus that used to operate out of Singapore. He might be the sort to amuse himself with this. There's also a Rumanian, Titus Telescu, who defected to Canada a year ago. A mis-chief-maker, very bright and dashing, but with a macabre sense of humor. His father was an agronomist, by the way. And his mother a chemo-biologist. His escapades are all on his dossier. The KGB would like to get their hands on him, but Telescu went into deep black, the moment he hit Canada. Out of sight."

Belmont said, "You're saving the third man for last."

"He's a part-Portuguese born in Goa, the former en-clave-colony in India. Then he went to Mozambique as chief security officer against the black terrorist rebels, and worked in Portuguese East Africa on a campaign that led the activists into one complicated trap after the other. He was remarkable. A devotee of gamesmanship. He never did anything the simple way. It was one devilish trick after the other: ambush, booby-trap, plot and counterplot."

"Does he have a name?"

"Colonel Paolo Bom Jesus da Santana. Short, built like a circus acrobat. Given to native women in various styles and outlandish techniques. Killed some of them sexually, I understand. His mother was a low-caste Indian woman with some English blood; his father was a petty clerk in the colonial service. No guessing where he came from. Before Santana went into intelligence, he ran whorehouses and gambling joints from Mozambique to Macao, and then Rio. The way he cleaned out the terrorists in Mozambique was by weird and brutal tortures. Call him amoral. Although he has a Portuguese name, he could really be anything. Willie Wells might know about him, since he was a mercenary in Africa for a couple of years. And as I said, I'm calling for a reliable team-member from Lisbon Central."

"Where do we pick up Willie?"

"In Ethiopia."

Wells always reminded Durell of a stalking black leopard, as intent on reaching his prey as any jungle animal, although he had been raised in Philadelphia ghettos, fought in Vietnam with distinction, then renounced the U.S for a time to drift around the world as a competent, deadly, efficient fighting man, offering his services to anyone and any cause, as long as the pay was sufficient. He had come to K Section through Durell, and Durell had good reason to respect the black man's capacities. They were friends—as friendly as Durell permitted himself to be with anyone in the business.

"Someone hung this on me," Wells said soberly, when they met at the hot, dusty airport, debarking from the Air Ethiopia 707. "I was in the market killing time, looking at what these locals produce. Bought a parchment painting, these three guys with spears." He showed Durell the yellowed scroll painted with a Byzantine style, showing three warriors in scarlet and yellow. "I didn't want it, but the stallkeeper practically shoved it at me for nothing. So I took it. Lo and behold, gentlemen! A message for the Cajun on the back."

Durell said, "So they spotted you, too?"

Belmont was angry. "Either they're mindreaders, or they've infiltrated our position—or we have a traitor working with us."

Andy Weyer clipped sun lenses over his horn-rimmed glasses and coughed delicately in the dust. His hair was long and unkempt, and he had assumed a stoop-shouldered posture. "Not necessarily. Durell thinks the paper chase is organized by someone who was once high up in the business. Somebody who works for the inventor of the Zero Formula. What does the message say?"

"We go to Johannesburg this afternoon."

Belmont said, "I'm getting a cramped butt from all these air hops."

"It's just begun, I think," Durell said.

## 5

From Johannesburg they were directed to fly to Tokyo. Durell no longer bothered to check out the messengers. They were either ignorant or innocent. Yet every step of the way had been meticulously planned for them on a timetable. In the third-rate Tokyo hotel to which they were directed, a message from Kevin Kendall and another from Charley Weintraub waited for them. Durell was not surprised that McFee was monitoring their global hops. The terms of the ultimatum concerning the Zero Formula had stipulated that no other K Section teams follow on Durell's heels; but local Centrals had kept track of them, when Durell reported in on his passage.

Kendall's message was pleasingly definitive:

"We have learned that among the alleged legitimate teams being sent to the auction—wherever it may be held —there are also two 'rogue' groups. One is a dissident faction from Red China, a splinter branch of war hawks from the Black House in Peking. They are headed by Po Tsutse, whom you doubtless know, and an Albanian as a front named Guerlan Stepanic. They are in Lisbon at the moment. The British are in Hong Kong, the Russians in Havana. The legitimate Chinese have not yet left Shanghai, where their team is assembled.

"The second rogue group is from Africa. I fear that the State Department's trust in Prince Tim as a balancing factor in the keystone independent black state of Pakuru has been disappointing and ill-founded. He has left Pakuru with his sister, the new Queen Elephant of Pakuru, and several of his mercenary intelligence people. Prince Tim has struck it rich, of course, with new finds of oil and diamond mines in his emerging nation. It seems to have gone to his head. His nation's ancient feud with the 'Neighbors' may be his motivation. Do not count on the fact that you once saved Atimboku's life. He has changed, and none for the better, I fear. Please be careful."

The second message was from Charley Weintraub, in K Section's laboratory:

Dossiers at K/NSA/DIA/FBI all negative. Negative from London G6 and Paris Surete and Interpol. Two repeat two possibilities: Paolo de Santana and Titus Telescu. No whereabouts defined. Biochemist Albert Hagen, Baltimore, and Soviet Science Award winner Josef P. V. Makornin, and British Lord Henry Rawdon, Nobel winner in wave-length studies to sterilize insect pests, and Japanese Hokutsi Okura all worked on life-wave modulation destruct projects. All men vanished. Take your pick, Cajun. Maybe all three. Maybe none. McFee says you are going to Brazil. Have fun with cucarachas.

Durell shared the messages with Wells, Andy Weyer and Belmont. None made any immediate comment. Wells was always quiet, impassive. Belmont simply looked annoyed. Andy Weyer opened a new box of nuts and raisins and said quietly,

"I'm being followed, Cajun."

Durell looked at his academic face. "By our people?"

"No. A Chinese. Two of 'em, as a matter of fact. Ugly characters. You told me to stick to you like a shin-plaster, but then you sent me to the Embassy for these messages, and that's where I was picked up."

"Did they follow you here?"

Weyer said simply, "I think they tried to kill me."

Belmont drew a deep breath. "Tell us, Andy."

"They were in one of these little Tokyo taxis. Kamikaze drivers, all right. I took our rented car around the Ginza, headed east toward the bay, took some counter-measures to shake them. They were like glue. Finally parked and went into a *pachinko* parlor to see what would happen. They stood in the doorway, watching. They didn't try to keep their surveillance in the black." Andy Weyer grinned. "So I called a cop."

Wells was startled. "You what?"

"I went up to a cop on the corner and asked him how to get back to this fleabag, using some of the Nisei Japanese I learned in California, one time. Then I pointed to the two Chinese. They were surprised, and vanished. But when I got back to the car, they were waiting. Two shots. Each had a pop at me. Both missed. So I ran. I mean, I jumped into the rental and took off like a cat with a firecracker on his tail. And got here okay."

Belmont wondered aloud, "Why you, Andy? It's Sam who carries the loot. He's the big Indian chief among us. So why did they pick on you?"

"I don't know," Weyer said.

Durell said, "The trails are coming together. They have to, eventually, in a day or two. Not all of the teams will have compunctions about wiping out the others to keep them from the auction."

A messenger knocked on the hotel-room door.

They were to leave at once on a flight over the Pacific, to Lima, Peru. For the first time, a two-lap directive was given. From Lima they were to fly over the Andes to Belém in Brazil.

Andy Weyer packed his bag and kept eating his nuts and raisins.

# Chapter Five

PARAMAQUITO sprawled under a steamy sun between the Amazon and the confluence of the Rio Xapajos, a broad tributary of copper-colored water that added its sullen torrent to the four-mile wide *O Rio Mar.* In 1910 the town had been a busy depot for the inland rubber plantations, enjoying a delirium of profit and bitter shame, instant fortunes made through the cruel exploitation of Indians who were little more than slaves. Two years later the boom collapsed when Southeast Asian plantations won the market with rubber taken from Amazon seeds. The *seringueros,* those tribesmen forced to work at gunpoint tapping the trees in the virgin forests, lapsed into dismal poverty—those who survived. Now the descendents of these *seringueros* lived in shanty towns built of palmetto matting, a few scraps of tin, and flattened oil drums. A miasma of despair hung over the slums.

Unlike Manaus, the bustling, resurgent city at the Rio Negro, which flowed into the Amazon with a mighty two-hundred-foot depth that flushed out forest and swamp, Paramaguito enjoyed no rebuilding, no skyscrapers, no new boom. Its once-elegant opera house reflected only crumbling splendor; its iron fishmarket, where Indian women offered *acara-acu, pira ricu,* and the giant *piraiba* catfish that sometimes reached 350 pounds, was a wide, hot area of stinking garbage, humming with green flies.

The steamboat docked under the sullen control of Manoel at the wheel, amid floating rafts of fishermen's canoes, all offering their wares in soft tones under the brazen morning sun. The mist had burned off the river. A youngster paddled his canoe under the main deck and offered slices of a giant anaconda he had trapped. Other Indians held up marmosets, cats, parrots, hawks, and dogs. On the dock, a man laid out finely woven hammocks for sale.

"Get some of those," Durell said to Wells. "Where is Agosto?"

"Coming," the black man said.

"And Belmont?"

"Tailing Stepanic. He went ashore with the first rush of passengers. You know how he feels about what happened to Andy in Belém. I'll pick up the hammocks, but I don't know what we want 'em for."

A girl who looked American in cut-off dungarees and a shirt with tails flapping over her buttocks waved to Durell and held up bamboo birdcages, one containing bright fly-catchers, some kiskadees, and a fierce harpy eagle, a bird the Indians referred to as winged wolves. Then she lowered the cages, grinned, and sat in the shade of a tin-sided waterfront shed on the dock. He noted her location, then saw Agosto come down the ladder from the main deck. Most of the passengers had already crowded down the gangway. The crew worked stolidly at unloading the meager cargo of the *Duos Irmãos*.

"How do you like it?" Agosto asked, smiling.

He had put on the khaki and red-pipped uniform of a Brazilian police colonel, with elegantly polished boots.

"You look the part, Agosto," Durell said.

"My credentials are in order. It may give us the clout you asked for." The brown eyes of the Brazilian slowly swung over the dock, came back, swung left again. "Who is the girl with the birds, senhor?"

"A friend, I hope. Arranged for her in Belém."

"You think of everything, Senhor Cajun."

Agosto's gray-streaked hair shone in the hot sun as he took off his cap and looked inside at nothing at all. His middle-aged face was solemn. His muscular chest heaved as he drew in a deep breath and put on sunglasses. "It stinks here."

"Tell us something new," Wells sighed.

"Yes. Well, O'Hara sneaked off the boat the moment we touched land. And Inocenza wants to talk to you, Cajun."

Durell nodded. "Right. You and Willie go to the Hotel *O Rei Felipe*. Wait for me. I'll be along soon."

Willie said, "You're carrying the letter of credit, Sam. We shouldn't leave you alone, Sam."

"Go ahead," Durell insisted. "Wait for Belmont at *O Rei Felipe*. I won't be gone for long."

## 2

Inocenza looked solemn and contrite, as beautiful as a dark, wind-grown orchid. In her plush, pink-lighted stateroom, she determinedly threw dresses, shoes, lingerie and boots into a battered suitcase. She wore old tennis shoes and tight-fitting slacks that emphasized the ripe contours of her rump. A white cotton bra held her firm breasts, and the gold chain with its crucifix delved between them. She had put a red bandana around her black hair, and her every move betrayed a resolution to carry out an important decision.

"Come in, Sam," she said, when he knocked.

"I'm sorry I had to do what I did last night."

She shook her head. "It is I who suffer *a dor*—sorrow. If I had understood you meant to do something bad to that ugly O'Hara, I would have helped you willingly. But I am finished here now. Nothing under *o céu*—the sky—could keep me on this boat any longer."

"What will you do, Inocenza?"

She stared, her dark skin glowing. "Am I not pretty?"

"Beautiful."

"You did not think so last night!"

"I did. But there was something else to be done."

"Ah, well. A pretty woman never has any problems in these river towns."

"You don't want to do that, Inocenza. Come with me."

"Oh? Now, you ask?"

"I still need your help. You can be paid for it."

"To work for you, Senhor Cajun? At what? I do not know if you are *o ladrão*—a thief—or a policeman, or what."

"I'm neither."

"What could I do? For a moment in my bed, I thought you were only *o mocó*—a boy. I know better, of course." She faced him, challengingly. "What do you want me to do?"

"Take me to where O'Hara stays in Paramaguito."

"No! Never, never, will I go back to that pig."

"Just take me to his place here?"

"You will be cruel to him?" she asked anxiously.

"If I have to be."

"Ah. Then I come with happiness to help you."


The girl with the birdcages still lingered on the dock. When she saw Durell on the gangway, she stood up and the harpy eagle screeched, its yellow eyes malevolent. The little kiskadee flycatchers in the other bamboo cages twittered in terror. The girl went into the rusty warehouse with her birds.

"You already have another lady-friend?" Inocenza asked.

"It's business."

"Ho. Ha. I do not like your job."

The girl in the cut-off jeans had taffy-colored hair and dirty bare feet. The warehouse smelled of fish and lumber and sawdust, stale food and bat droppings.

"Hi. I'm Connie Drew," she said. "You're the Cajun, right? I used to be here in the Peace Corps. A real grump. When we were all fired, I stayed on, teaching the Indians in shanty-town."

"I know. We've kept track of you."

"We? I didn't think anybody cared what I was doing." She was suddenly hostile. "So who's keeping an eye on me? Are you Big Brother?"

"In a way. Just cool it, Connie. We need your help for a bit. Did you get the GK-12 transceiver flown in to you from Belém?"

"Sure. I can work it, too. Who is 'we'?"

"Uncle Sam, if you want to call it that."

"Hell."

"Me, if you prefer."

She eyed him. "You don't look too awful."

"All we want you to do is monitor the GK-12 for a few days. You should be getting a message from me, I hope."

She was suspicious. "You with the oil people? The Companhia Meridional de Mineraçao? They're doing a geological survey inland with some snappy new radar stuff that can look sidewise and see through clouds. They say there are iron-ore deposits up the Rio Xapajos, which is why it runs red, they say."

"Could be."

"But you're not, are you? You're looking for somebody?"

"Connie, if in three days or so, I ask for help, like a plane, can you get one in to me?"

"Depends, if it can land where you happen to be."

"There will be a hundred dollars in it for you."

"Hell, you can shove your bribe, mister. My ass!"

"The Indian kids you teach might be able to use it."

"Oh." She grinned. "You're a tricky s.o.b., I can see that. Make it two hundred, in that case. You must be loaded."

"It's a deal."

"Want to buy one of my birds?"

Durell looked at the vicious harpy eagle. "No, thanks."


# 3


The place was a mile upriver on the outskirts of Paramaguito. The morning sun made it an inferno. Flies and mosquitos and a hundred other varieties of insects, oversized and overly aggressive, buzzed, swarmed, hopped and clicked in the thick saw grass along the path. A battered taxi had taken them to the end of the dusty road leading out of town. The Rio Xapajos was a vast rust-red stream moving sluggishly toward the overpowering Amazon at their rear. Smoke from brush fires stained the pale sky.

A rusty Coca-Cola sign hung from the shack at the end

of the path. An equally rusty jeep was decaying under the onslaughts of humidity, orchid vines, and chewing insects.

"He comes here to see a woman," Inocenza said.

"What woman?"

"More Indian than me. Big and fat. He gets drunk."

On the water's edge, where a rickety dock had collapsed into the reddish current, a large corrugated iron shed, surrounded by a broken web fence, was almost indistinguishable from the forest and swamps beyond. The sound of a tinny radio came from within the cavernous interior. He smelled manioc pancakes frying, and realized he was hungry. None of them had had breakfast. The big shed had once been a rubber processing plant, where the smoked rubber, in days gone by, had been delivered here in great balls of two hundred pounds each. The past was dead and decayed here.

"What do you want from O'Hara?" Inocenza asked.

"Information."

"He knows what you must know? If he does not tell you, what will you do?"

"He'll tell me," Durell said grimly.

"He is a dangerous man. Be careful. I want to go with you, though. I want to watch."

Durell looked at her. There was a strange light in her smoky eyes. "Do you hate him so much, Inocenza? I won't kill him just to please you, you know."

She smiled grimly. "Perhaps I will be lucky."

He moved toward the shed. He thought he saw a caiman in the reddish river that swirled around the broken dock. He looked back, but no one had followed them out of town. Inocenza moved lightly beside him. Her breathing had quickened. He pushed aside some vines and stepped through the wide, yawning doorway.

"O'Hara!" he called into the darkness.

His voice echoed eerily. There were piles of bat droppings on the cracked concrete. No one answered him. He heard the radio playing a swift Brazilian tune. Probably from Manaus, he thought. Daylight shone in gloomy shafts through holes in the roof. More daylight showed at the opposite end of the warehouse. The place smelled of the bats, of ancient sweat, of smoky rubber, even after all these years. Machinery stood in broken shapes here and there. Vines came down through the holes in the roof.

He took out his gun.

Then he heard O'Hara's voice, rumbling, half-singing. It came from the opposite end of the long shed. He ducked through the interior vines and came onto a stilt cabin supported on raw poles, with woven reed sides and an old iron stove and a mildewed mattress on the dirty floor. Through the three open sides, he could see the wide river.

O'Hara sprawled in an Indian hammock, a bottle of Tepucata beer in his hand, a number of empties on the dirt floor around him. The Indian woman knelt naked on her haunches, her enormous, flaccid buttocks spread, and cooked the manioc cakes Durell had smelled in the warehouse. A faded, flowered dress lay on the dirt floor beside her. Her pendulous breasts swung as she turned to look at Durell when he stepped in. She held a new, shiny spatula in her left hand. The charcoal fire was smoky. The place stank of sweat and O'Hara. There was a bruise on the Indian woman's flat face. Nothing changed in her solemn, patient face. Her eyes were just eyes.

"O'Hara!" Durell said.

The fat, bearded man was singing remotely in tune with the battery radio. His voice was hoarse, bawdy. His bald head shone just above the edge of the sagging hammock. Durell called his name again and the man kept singing and waving the beer bottle over his head. The naked old Indian woman crouched and watched with limpid, sorrowing eyes. Durell crossed the shack, caught one edge of the hammock, and flipped it over. O'Hara crashed mountainously to the floor. His roar of rage made the Indian woman sit backward on her vast buttocks. The beer bottle broke. O'Hara came up with his Colt's Frontiersman swinging toward Durell. There was nothing drunken in his rheumy eyes. Durell kicked at the gun and knocked it across the floor and it landed at the Indian woman's knees. She did not move to touch it. O'Hara lunged for it and Durell kicked him in the flank and O'Hara went over, rolling on his beer-keg belly. He wore stained, striped cotton

pants, nothing more. He went for the gun again and Durell
kicked it from between the Indian woman's knees. Inocenza picked it up and said, "*Capitáo,* if you move, I will
blow a hole through your big belly."

"Inocenza, what—"

"I mean it."

"I know you mean it, baby."

"Then be still. Do not bother *a mãe* anymore."

Durell said, "She's your mother?"

O'Hara made a spitting sound. "Shit. She's nobody's
mother. You'd be surprised who Inocenza's mother really
was."

Durell said, "Move over there, O'Hara. Pull up your
pants."

O'Hara said, "She's seen the engine before."

"You're not drunk, so you can understand me. You're
going to answer a few questions."

"You need Inocenza to help you?"

"I wouldn't stop her. Where are the rest of your clothes?"

"*A mãe* is washing them."

"Inocenza, tell her to get them. O'Hara, you'll get
dressed and come with me."

O'Hara rubbed his bald head, pulled at his unkempt
beard, and whined, "I'm an old man. You're pickin' on an
old man who don't know anything. Why, I'm as old as
your grandpappy Jonathan—takin' off ten years, maybe. I
can't tell you nothing. I keep forgettin' things, lately. Gettin' senile, maybe." O'Hara spat and belched. Durell could
smell the stale beer on his breath. The manioc cakes were
starting to burn when Inocenza spoke softly to the Indian
woman, who got up and put on her faded cotton dress
over her bulbous body. Then she went out quietly. Inocenza scraped the burned manioc off the heated griddle.
O'Hara said, "Regular little homemaker, ain't you, baby?
Any man can find a home between your legs."

Durell hit him, snapping his head aside, and O'Hara fell
against the hammock. He hung there, arms spread, his
head lowered. He spat blood from his lower lip. Durell
said, "Tell me now. Tell me who you're working for."

"And if I don't?"

"Then I'll kill you."

"And then you won't get to the auction."

"I'm breaking the string. I'm on my own now. I'll get there," Durell said, "with or without you."

"To hell with you," O'Hara said.

"Inocenza?"

"Yes, Senhor Sam."

"Kill him," Durell said. "Any way you like."

"Yes, Senhor Sam."

The black-haired girl raised O'Hara's big gun. Her almond eyes gleamed like hot coals. Her smile was crooked as her finger tightened on the trigger. O'Hara screamed and ran back behind the hammock as if it could offer him protection. His bristly gray beard quivered.

"Hold it," Durell told the girl.

She looked disappointed.

"Now tell me," Durell said.

O'Hara belched again. "I don't know his name. His place is up the Xapajos—maybe twenty, thirty miles. All I know is I got this money, the passage for you and your people, and Mr. Stepanic and his people, and I was told to take you upriver until I'd be told to stop and let you off."

"Where?"

"I don't know. He never said."

"What did he look like?"

"All I saw was a young squirt, a messenger."

"What's up the river?"

"Nothing," O'Hara said sullenly. "I only go as far as Tiparucu. That's maybe forty miles upstream. It's an old railroad terminus. Death Railway, they used to call it, in the old rubber days. Them were good times, lots of money around, everybody working, like a gold rush."

"What did this messenger look like?"

O'Hara coughed. "Could I have another beer?"

"No. Answer me."

"Just one of these slick hip Indian boys who went to Belém and Rio and learned reading. I got no other answers for you, Durell. Anyway, his money spoke for him. I need the beer real bad. You're real cruel to an old man. I've told you all the truth I know."

"What happens at the Hotel *O Rei Felipe?*"

"You get orders to stay on the *Irmãos* with me."

"As far as Tiparucu?"

"That's right."

"Any other passengers?"

O'Hara looked devious. "A couple. I seen them already. They had bad luck. Their hydroplane crashed. They're blacks, strange people. From Africa, I think."

"You're supposed to take them, too?"

"Correct."

Durell drew a deep breath. He knew O'Hara was not telling all of the truth. The Indian woman came back and handed O'Hara his damp clothes. The sun was up over the treetops now. The reddish silt in the river made it look stained with blood. He suppressed a quick rush of anger.

"You admitted you know we're going to an auction, O'Hara. How do you know about it?"

"The guy with the money said that."

"What's being auctioned?"

"I don't know and I purely don't care. I take you where you're supposed to go, I got my money and another five thousand when we get there, and that's all." O'Hara hopped on one foot, putting on his shoes. "Inocenza, baby, stop pointin' that big old gun at your papa."

"You're not my papa, you old goat."

"I sure ain't, but I raised you since you stopped suckin' your mother's tit. I fed you and taught you good, all about the river. So put away that gun."

Durell said, "Let's go."

"Where?" O'Hara asked. "I got to look after my boat."

"You go where I say, from now on."

## 4

Willie Wells was waiting at the Hotel *O Rei Felipe.* "Did you spot Belmont? That crazy bastard is still hunting for Stepanic. Stepanic vanished off the boat and he sure hasn't come here. But we've got other company, Cajun."

"Where is Agosto?"

"Taking a shower. His colonel's uniform worked like a charm." Willie looked at Inocenza. "Hi."

"Hello," said the girl.

"Sam treating you right?"

"Just fine."

"You could be my girl, any time," Wells said.

"Take it easy, Willie," Durell said.

"Well, I always went for her color."

"Any messages? No new directives?"

"Nothing yet. Do we just sit here?"

"No," Durell said. "Take care of O'Hara, will you? See if you can sober him up."

"You want some breakfast, Sam?"

"In a little while."

He went looking for the company Wells had mentioned. The hotel was a sprawling affair with Victorian gingerbread that looked riddled with termites; it had a wide, musty lobby curtained in deep gloom and a long veranda in the rear facing the river. A few American roadworkers already sat at the bar. There were globe lamps, revolving fans in the ceiling, tasseled draperies from the turn of the century. The hotel was not crowded. Durell made a few inquiries of the Portuguese clerk at the desk, then went up the broad stairway from the lobby to the upper corridor, which was shadowed and cool compared to the sticky heat outside. They were not far from the ornate iron galleries of the fish market, slightly nostalgic of New Orleans.

The room was wide and airy, overlooking the junction of the two vast rivers. A small balcony gave him a glimpse of the docks to the left, with the twin stacks of the *Duos Irmãos* half a mile to the north, amid fishing boats and oil barges. A pall of humid mist hung over the view. Far across the rivers, the forests of the Amazon made a gray-green smudge against the hot, pale sky. There was not a cloud to be seen.

"You can just see it past the bend," Agosto said. He had come out of the tiled bathroom, resplendent in his police colonel's uniform. "They broke a pontoon. Hit some driftwood."

The hydroplane lay canted in the water, one wing

tipped toward the sky. No one was near it. The nose was buried in debris that floated on the copper-tinted water.

Agosto smiled gently. "I checked the local police headquarters. My credentials worked very well, Senhor Sam. They say it flew in from Recife. The people in it are Africans."

"So I heard. Where are they staying?"

"Right here, Senhor Sam." The stocky Portuguese from Belém looked at Durell curiously. "The senhora—very lovely—asked for you at once. I checked their papers. All in order, visas, no contraband, but of course I am sure they all have arms. Their names are—"

"Prince Atimboku, Salduva Hukkim, and assorted assassins."

"Ah. You know them?"

"I know them," Durell said grimly.

"The African girl is very beautiful, I must say."

"Sally is all right; but Prince Tim worries me. He has a crazy violence, Agosto, that could blow us all sky-high."

"I checked everything, senhor," Agosto said. "They occupy a room above us. They have two—ah—warriors with them. They look uncomfortable in Western clothes. They are each seven feet tall—the warriors, I mean. The woman—the girl—is called the Queen Elephant of Pakuru."

"Royalty," Durell said. "I'd better see them."

"Are they competitors?"

"Rogues."

"They have money for the auction, too?"

"Diamond mines. Copper. A whole nation."

Agosto smoothed his small black moustache. "You wish to go alone, I see. I shall wait here for Belmont."

Durell nodded. "Willie is down in the lobby. He'll be bringing up Captain O'Hara and Inocenza. O'Hara is our ace."

Agosto smiled. "As you wish, Senhor Sam."

# 5

He saw her the moment he stepped into the corridor. A fine brass wall clock out there read nine o'clock. She came down the steps at the end of the hall with a quick, light stride and he saw her golden eyes and the big hooped earrings and her fine, small head and the gay skirt of striped Pakuru design, and for a moment he went back somewhere else, to Africa, to a railroad and a time of love and a time of danger, when he had saved her brother who was trying to assert his hereditary rights to the tribal throne of the emerging nation of Pakuru. All in the moment, he remembered their nights together after he got Prince Atimboku Mari Mak Mujilikaka safely free to plead for his rights at the United Nations. He and Sally had then spent two weeks in a Mozambique town by the Indian Ocean, smiled at by the Portuguese as lovers. Later, she became the "Queen Elephant" on the death of her matriarch mother. He shook his head. There were too many memories. It was over three years since he had last seen Sally, but she looked lovelier than ever, golden-eyed, radiantly exotic with her copper skin that reflected the blend of her mixed inheritance, part Boer, Chinese, and Banda. The only thing she had in common with her brother Prince Tim was her dark hair, carefully braided and massed above her regal face, since Atimboku had inherited from his father's Banda wife the fine aquiline features and ebony skin of the Banda people.

"Sam?" Sally whispered. "Darling Cajun?"

She came down the stairs in an impetuous rush, then checked herself. She smiled. The hotel corridor was silent.

"Hello, Salduva."

"Tim said you would be here. He said no one else but you would be chosen."

"It's good to see you, Salduva."

"Please call me Sally. The way you used to."

They stood a few feet apart. At first glance, nothing was

changed. She had been three years and worlds away. Now only a step or two, and a moment, separated them. Durell took her arm and tuned into an angle of the corridor and they were out on the balcony that overlooked the river. She looked cool and competent, but he had hoped she wouldn't be here. He did not want her to be a part of this. Her hand was cool in his.

"You don't wish to kiss me, darling Sam?"

"You're royalty now." He smiled. "Do you still share the government with Prince Tim?"

"My brother would still like to kill me."

"Has he tried?"

Her smile was thin. "Not lately. He wanted to keep me from this—this gruesome auction. I came along to stop him. He means to buy the formula, Sam. It was tested and demonstrated in our country, too, you know. Tim is uncountably rich. He's built a few schools, some new roads, a great government palace where the tribal *kraals* used to be. But he keeps most of the national income for himself. He—he *owns* Pakuru, lock, stock and barrel."

Durell's voice was edged with anger. "Yes, thanks to our State Department, which made a pet of him."

"He's much worse now, darling Sam. He'll sell the whole country into slavery for the formula." She shook her head, and the big hoops of gold at her ears sparkled. "His bodyguard goes everywhere with him. His killers." She paused again. "He says that now our plane is smashed, he'll hitch a ride with you."

"No," Durell said.

"He will. You wouldn't know him now. He held his promise once, but—oh, I wish I were back in England, writing those stupid articles for that silly old magazine, *Toward Sunshine!* I wish—but then I'd never have met you, would I? I remember—so much."

"Yes."

No one else was on the veranda. There was a steady hubbub of sound from the fishmarket, the chugging of a tug that pushed another oil barge into its wharf downstream.

"Sam, Prince Tim will kill you. He considers you his

most dangerous opposition. I told you, he wants the formula, and nothing will stop him. Please, please be careful."

"I'll go see him," Durell said. "He's still only a spoiled brat, to me."

"You're wrong. He's a man, cruel and ruthless. I tell you he has changed, and he will not be stopped—"

"I'll stop him," Durell said.

She clung to him. "I should have stayed with you and never gone back from Mozambique. I should never have left you."

He said gently, "Sally, you belong to Pakuru. It's your country. You're its only hope."

She shook her head. "I can't beat Tim."

"We'll see."

## 6

No one had been in the corridor when he first took Sally out on the veranda, but when he stepped back into the gloomy hall, they were waiting for him, two of them, lean and immensely tall, very black, their knives very long and sharp.

They stood flat against the wall of the wide double-leafed door Durell went through. Their knives pricked his sides and one of them said in a careful Cambridge accent, "Be very still and silent, Mr. Durell." He did not move. They were Bandas from Pakuru, to judge from the tribal scars that beaded their long, bony faces. They wore their Western clothing as if they were the tentlike tribal cloaks of Africa. Each man towered well over seven feet in height.

Sally, behind him, sharply ordered them to put down their knives. Durell said calmly, "Don't worry, they're not going to kill me."

"Not yet, Mr. Durell. Come with us, please."

"To Prince Tim?"

"Prince Atimboku Mari Mak Mujilikaka, yes. Do not be impertinent to the Lion of Lions. Come."

Durell felt the impatience in the warriors; they were very intense, which was peculiarly gratifying. He nodded and said, "Fine," to the first assassin and then took one step forward, which put them a little behind him, and then he turned quickly, chopping with both hands at the knives that pointed laterally now, for just that instant, at his back. The right-hand blow broke a wrist; his left hit the dark strong fingers holding the second knife. It sent the shining weapon in a twinkling blur across the scruffy corridor carpet. Sally made a quick yelping sound, unbecoming to her royal station. The man with the broken wrist howled and turned aside. Durell hit him low in the back and drove him into the opposite wall with a thump. The second man swung, his great height a handicap now, and Durell ducked under the hammerlike blow and straightened, kneed him, and sent him doubling up. Sally screamed something. Durell scooped up the knife on the floor and came up behind the first man and pricked the point just under the African's ear, drawing blood.

"One move," he said quietly, "And your throat is opened like a pig to be slaughtered. Do you understand?"

The man hissed. "Yes. Ngumi?"

The other Pakuran was on all fours, holding his broken wrist. "I hear."

"This man is Durell, Ngumi. We will kill him later."

Great beads of sweat stood out on the bony face of Ngumi as he held his wrist. "If you will permit us, sir—"

"I permit nothing." Durell looked at Sally's golden face. No one in O Rei Philipe had been disturbed.

Prince Tim had gained weight since his radical college days at Yale, when he went barefooted and played a flute. He had been a lean and handsome youth then, a powerful man when Durell had helped him escape from Pakuru to claim his royal rights. Now he had gone to seed. His face was still handsome, black and aquiline like most Bandas, a startling contrast to his half-sister with her Boer and Chinese blood; but there was a fleshiness to the jawline, a hint of pouches under his ever-angry eyes, a sense of fat around the middle. He had enjoyed the booming prosperi-

ty of Pakuru when copper and diamond mines were discovered, making himself virtually a dictator among the
restless nations of the Organization of African Unity. The
violence in his angry mind had not ended with his assump-
tion of ruthless power.

"You have not changed, Mr. Durell."

"But you have, Tim."

"Ah. My little paunch? I eat well, remembering my
hungry days. Is that Salduva with you?"

Sally stood behind Durell, and the two warriors looked
bent and broken in the hotel-room doorway. Atimboku
had chose a suite on the third floor and made himself comfortable. He looked in contempt at his two men and ordered the one with a broken wrist to find a doctor. Atimboku wore a white suit of Shantung silk, with a striped
shirt open at the collar, leather English boots, an Egyptian
scarab ring. He lolled back in a Bombay chair and grinned
at Durell.

"Many things have changed, in addition to my waist-
line. Of course you know that Pakuru, my once-impov-
erished little country, is now wealthy beyond anyone's
dreams. We can now *export* money, so to speak, to
achieve our aims."

"Yes," Durell said, "I know you finance mercenary terrorists against the Portuguese in Mozambique and sabo-
tage against the Ndohuzas, your so-called Neighbors."

"One must implement foreign policy for the benefit of
the nation," Atimboku said.

"So you've come here to bid for the Zero Formula?"

"I shall buy it. Nothing can stop me."

"And you'll sell Pakuru back into poverty?"

"The formula will achieve all things for us."

"And horror for the Neighbors?"

"They deserve to be destroyed." Atimboku smiled. "I
never really liked you, Durell. I expect you want me to be
appreciative for helping me several years ago. I thank you
for it. But I never liked you. You never wanted me to rule
Pakuru. But now we shall bid against each other, and I
shall win in this bidding, rest assured. You will take me to
the auction, and Sally will give me all the help I need

against you. I understand you Americans; I know your strengths and weaknesses. I was educated among you. You are too romantic, too naïve, too susceptible to idealism in a world hostile to you." He clenched his fist on his knee. "You will be mine, Durell."

It was 9:30 when he returned to his own room on the second floor. Captain O'Hara was asleep, snoring on one of the four beds in the huge room. He smelled even worse than before. Agosto was eating a breakfast of eggs, ham, and manioc bread. Willie Wells sat tilted in a chair beside the door, his face hard and angry. The sound of the tepid shower in the big tiled bathroom told Durell where Inocenza was. He pointed to O'Hara's snoring figure.

"Roll him out of bed. We're going to the boat and heading upriver, right now."

Agosto waved his fork and said mildly, "Belmont has not come back yet, Senhor Sam."

"He hasn't called in?"

"He has an itch, senhor, to kill. He is still hunting for Stepanic in this town. He surely has not succeeded. And he has not yet returned."

Willie Wells said grimly, "I think Stepanic got him— just like Stepanic got Andy Weyer in Belém."

# Chapter Six

DURELL remembered Belém. It was where Agosto had been recruited to join their team. And where Andy Weyer had died in such an ugly fashion.

The city of *Nossa Senhora de Belém,* the Lady of Bethlehem, commanded the many mouths of the giant Amazon, and its harbor was clogged with freighters that came ninety miles up the Para River to serve the area. In spite of the traffic jams at the rush hour and the green parks that separated bright, towering skyscrapers, it was a city of sweet scents, with oases of colonial quiet and charm. It was the cultural capital of northern Brazil, grown to well over half a million people since it was first founded by Portuguese adventurers in 1616.

They had been directed to check into the Grao Pará Excelsior, after their flight from Tokyo and Peru. They had dinner at the Hotel Vanja, eating *pato no tucupi,* a duck soup that warmed the stomach long after dinner. Nobody seemed to be following them, although Andy Weyer was a bit jumpy. He did not go with them to dinner. He ate his nuts and raisins, and then picked up a bowl of tacacá, a hot soup served by sidewalk venders who used painted gourds for plates. Afterward, to check surveillance, Durell and Wells walked down the crowded Praça da Repubblica, with its looming statues in turn-of-the-century style, the parks where youngsters played *futeball,* and the shills offering Cessna rides to Marajó Island to see the herds of water buffalo. When they returned to the Grao Pará Excelsior, there was still no message directing them to the next destination.

Weyer wondered what came next. "I think we're close, Sam. According to the time schedule, there aren't too many days left before this alleged auction."

Belmont said, "First time there hasn't been a directive waiting for us." He had bought some thin Brazilian cigars and he lit one now, the match flaring in the equatorial afternoon sun. The room was air-conditioned and comfortable against the humid heat outside. The sound of traffic down below made a pervasive hum. "I agree with Andy. We're getting near."

Willie Wells said, "Maybe, without a new note, we're being told to jump through a hoop."

"Take it easy, all of you," Durell said. "Andy, our Central here isn't much—a little shop off the Praça da Repubblica. Sells tourist stuff—Amazon skins, caiman leather, Indian things. The man's name is Velho. Maybe he has a message for us. Go there and see Velho—and check out if you're still being tailed."

Belmont said, "Andy's supposed to stick with you, Sam. I'll do it."

Durell shook his head. "Let's pull some teeth, if Andy has a tiger following him."

The shop was closed. A sign in the window announced it would open again at six. It was only five o'clock. Restive, Weyer clipped sun-lenses over his horn-rimmed glasses and stared into the dusty window, with its jumble of tourist junk and reflections of passersby. The place was near the Tapa Taloca, a restaurant popular with the Belémese, decorated like a thatched Indian hut and huddled between tall business buildings. Traffic hooted and tires screeched in the busy rush hour. Not far off was the Bosque, a public garden saved from the original jungle. Weyer felt a prickling sensation on the nape of his neck. He was wearing dungarees, a flapping white shirt, and sandals. Except for his height and coloring, which proclaimed him as a North American, he had done nothing to attract attention.

But a small yellow Toyota had circled the block twice, passing him.

He could not see who was in it.

He rapped on the shop door, but the steel shutters were down, and after waiting another minute, he turned and walked away. Strapped to his right calf was a six-inch knife. Under the flapping white shirt whose tails he wore out over his slacks, he carried a flat .32 Beretta, pressed hard against his stomach. He did not know why he should feel uneasy. He joined the throngs back on the Praça da Repubblica, and turned toward the Bosque. The chatter of amiable Portuguese surrounded him. The flowering trees filled the hot evening air with a sweet scent. The yellow Toyota rounded the corner once more. The sun glared on its windshield. He did not see it again.

In the gardens, he deliberately took paths through the densest foliage and along the reflecting pools covered with big water lilies. Flat-faced Indian women with obedient children in white and a few businessmen and lovers strolled here. The lovers made Andy Weyer feel suddenly lonely.

In half an hour he emerged and saw the man in the white straw hat waiting for him. He took a taxi to the docks at Ver o Péso and wandered through the market, looking at the fishing boats. It was almost six o'clock. He saw the white Panama twice more. He used evasive tactics, testing gently. The man was good at his job, but he could not know if the tail was aware that he knew of the surveillance. He wondered if it was assumed he was Durell. He considered calling the hotel and stepped into a booth at the entrance of Ver o Péso and then stepped out again.

"Come along," the man said. "We have played enough with each other, eh?"

Weyer poked up his glasses. He was getting sunburned, and his face was sensitive. "Where do you want to go?"

"You will see."

"Do you know me?"

"I know you."

"Are you fuzz?"

"No fuzz. Not exactly. Come."

The weapon the man pressed against the lower lumbar region of Weyer's spine was a persuasive argument. Andy didn't mind. You never learned anything by ducking out, he thought.

The yellow Toyota was parked a short walking distance from the waterfront market. The lights were coming on in Belém's skyscrapers. Dusk gathered in the streets and alleys. The man seemed pleasant enough, except for his gun. But Andy felt capable of beating him. The man was short and stocky, perhaps in his late forties, with a bland olive face, not quite Portuguese. And the accent was of an oddly mixed origin. He had a pleasant, mature expression, with intelligent, careful eyes.

"Have you got me confused with Durell?" he asked.

"Get in the car. Please do nothing foolish."

"Have you a message for us?"

"We will go back to the shop where you were waiting."

"Are you from Central?"

The man ignored him and started the Toyota and drove back toward the center of the city, deftly weaving his way through the traffic. The restaurants were beginning to open, but the major patronage would not come for three hours yet. Andy relaxed, but not too much. He was aware of his gun pressing against his belly, of the knife strapped to his right leg. No sweat. He said, "Have you a name?"

"I will tell it to you soon."

"I could jump out of the car," Andy suggested.

"Then you will not learn what you must learn."

"So you do have a message for Durell? If you do, let's go to the hotel."

"No. The shop. Don't worry about anything, Andy."

"Then why do you use a gun against me?"

Again the pleasant, middle-aged man ignored him. There was an alley behind the shop and an iron-grilled gate to the right. The man parked and took out a key and gave it to Andy. He kept his gun in his lap, a heavy Browning with a silencer on it. "Please unlock the gate for me. We will put the car inside. One cannot find a place for a car here unless one has a private area for it."

Weyer did as he was told. The heavy gate swung inward and the man drove the Toyota through. It was growing dark now. He could have escaped down the alley then and there. But the man spoke softly and Andy felt he could take command whenever he wished. There were flowering

shrubs in the tiny garden. The man called to him and
Andy came through the gate and closed it and returned
the key.

"Thank you, senhor."

They went into the building by the back way.

"You first," the stranger said.

He looked like an amiable shopkeeper. K Section always chose such innocuous types. Andy went ahead into a
back room, a kitchen, he thought, although the gloom was
too deep to see distinctly. The gun prodded him again.
Unnecessary, Andy thought. You're too careful, old
buddy.

"Please go up the stairs," the man said. "Be careful, do
not stumble. I would rather not put on any lights."

The stranger's footsteps made no sound on the wooden
treads behind him. Andy made a note that the man was
light and quick on his feet. There was a smell in the air as
if a toilet had overflowed. A door opened. A faint light
came in from the street lights in front of the small building. He smelled cooking and saw the gleam of metal from
a radio transmitter and felt better, since it was standard
equipment for a K Section Central.

"Go ahead," the man said, pushing with his gun.

"Put that thing away," Andy said.

"*Sim.* Yes. In a moment. When I see your papers. One
must be careful, eh? A lot of money is involved."

"I don't have any money on me."

"*Sim.* I know. Go in, please."

He saw the dead man first. The body sprawled across a
green metal desk with a gooseneck lamp shining on the
bullethole behind the man's left ear. The victim had been
bald, plump, wearing a shabby shopkeeper's coat and
scuffed, pointed shoes. He looked as if he had been shot
while sitting in the swivel chair behind the desk. He hadn't
much of a face left, from what Weyer could see, since the
bullet had come out the right side of his round head, blowing away teeth, brains, cheekbone, and flesh in a wide
spatter over the edge of the desk and on the floor.

Weyer drew a deep breath.

"The shopkeeper?"

*"Sim."*

"No wonder you were careful."

*"Sim."*

"Who did it?" Andy asked.

"I did," said the man, and shot Andy in the back.

The shock of the bullet slammed through his right kidney and out through the lower right front quadrant of his stomach. He felt as if he had been struck with a poleaxe. He went down on all fours, knocking his head against a corner of the bloody desk, then plowing the dusty, stained carpet with his face. Dimly, conscious that he was badly wounded, not yet questioning why, Andy tried for the knife strapped to his right calf, but his reflexes were slow, nonexistent, and the man kicked at him, then stamped on his wrist and broke the bones in there and then kicked him again and rolled him over on his back. He felt no pain yet. He knew only numbness. The gooseneck lamp on the desk glared into his eyes. The man who had shot him stood over him, looking enormous, yet still mild, smiling with his gentle mouth, his eyes almost sorrowing.

"It is too bad, senhor."

Andy made vague movements with his left hand, toward the gun in his belt under his white shirt which was white no longer. "Why?" he whispered.

"It is necessary. You were overconfident, eh?"

"Son of—a bitch—"

The man broke his left arm, kneeling down beside him to do it. He worked meticulously, expertly. He knew how to hurt, but Andy was beyond hurt. He felt the gun ripped from his belt, and the zipper of his slacks came undone and the man clucked and took the knife from its sheath on Andy's leg and quickly, expertly, emasculated him. This time he felt the pain and opened his mouth to scream, but there was blood on his tongue and he knew he had bitten halfway through it. The man then took the knife and jabbed it into Andy's throat and quickly sawed back and forth, jumping back as the blood spurted.

There was nothing more he could do to Andy that Andy Weyer would ever know about.

The middle-aged man stood up with a sigh, carefully avoiding the blood now spattered and puddled around Weyer's ruined body. He pressed his gun into the hand of the man sprawled on the desk, the K Section Control who ran the souvenir shop downstairs. The smell of feces and urine in the room increased sharply. From the desk, the assassin took a few papers and cards, carefully put them in his pocket, then wiped the desk and the doorknob with a cloth taken from one of the desk drawers, and then very meticulously flicked the cloth over his pointed shoes, restoring them to a high, pleasing polish.

He picked up the telephone and dialed the Hotel *Grao Pará Excelsior* and soon got the room he wanted.

His voice was gentle.

"Senhor Durell?"

"Yes."

"Ah. I am sorry to have been a little late. My instructions are to join you—your team, *sim?* I am the man from Lisboa. But there has been an unfortunate event here in the Central. Your friend, Senhor Weyer, has been killed. It is a dangerous assignment we are on, is it not so? It is very shocking."

Durell's voice crackled harshly. "Andy is dead? Who is this?"

"Why, you asked especially for me to join your team, senhor. My name is Agosto. Agosto Laurentino de Mello. Agosto, senhor. I shall come to you at once."

# Chapter Seven

"ANDA NÃO," Agosto said quietly. "Not yet. Shall I go to the police and look for him? I can use my credentials."

"No," Durell said. "Belmont has to take care of himself. Manoel, let's shove off."

"*Sim,* senhor."

The young pilot turned his bruised face away. Agosto took one of his thin cigars from his natty uniform pocket and watched the docks of Paramaguito. At eleven in the morning, the waterfront was crowded with fishermen, vendors, wandering animals. A small crowd of hopeful passengers looked disconsolate as the *Duos Irmãos* shuddered, bell ringing, and the big paddlewheels began to churn and open the distance between the vessel and the wharf. The engine gang and deck crew went about their duties with Indian stolidity, asking no questions. Manoel had decided to cooperate, as long as Inocenza was aboard. They had taken on some freight, but the second-class passenger quarters on the main deck was empty of the usual hammocks, crates, wives, children and livestock. They had the ship to themselves.

"Where are we going?" Wells asked quietly.

"I know part of the way. We'll find out the rest."

Wells' dark face was angry. "I wouldn't trust that old *capitão* farther than I could punch his old lard-belly. He hates your guts, Sam. And do you know why?"

"I'm beginning to guess."

"It's something personal, going way back, right?"

"I think so," Durell said.

Wells sighed. "Small world, to coin a phrase."

"Is O'Hara sober yet?"

"*Anda não,* as Agosto says. Not yet."

One of the Indian crew came up the ladder to the Texas

deck where they were gathered. He checked himself at sight of Agosto's trim police colonel's uniform, then spoke to Manoel in a rapid flow of Indian, pointing over the bow. The man was naked to the waist and wore a silver crucifix and a pagan Indian charm on a chain. He looked undernourished. Agosto spoke sharply to him and the Indian stopped chattering, but kept his finger pointed forward.

A steam launch came around the first bend of the river. They were just opposite the verandas and tall windows of the Hotel *O Rei Felipe.* There were uniforms on the steam launch and the sound of its horn hooted over the hot, flashing water. Manoel responded by pulling on the *Duos Irmãos'* whistle. Then he rang the engine room to halt.

"It is the police, senhor." He looked at Agosto. "This man is maybe not police. They demand that we stop."

"Can you handle it?" Durell asked Agosto.

Agosto shrugged. "It would seem odd if we resisted their order. We must stop to see what they want. I can bluff it."

"I know that they want," Durell said grimly. "I see their passengers. Atimboku has brought in the local constabulary."

The launch came alongside with a rush of foam. Its squat funnel gave off oppresive fumes in the hot morning air. Durell and Agosto went down the ladder to the main deck. The steamboat's paddles hung dripping and motionless in their coverings. Inocenza opened her cabin door, looked at him and Agosto, and abruptly retreated inside. Her face was angry and jealous the moment when she glimpsed Sally Hukkim step lightly aboard.

Agosto spoke sharply, "One moment, Lieutenant."

The police officer on the launch saluted sloppily. He needed a shave. But the flap over his holstered gun was loose.

"Senhor Colonel, it is my duty to put these people aboard the steamboat. We have been ordered—"

"This boat is requisitioned by the provincial government," Agosto said. "It is now on government duty. Stand clear and keep your passengers off, Lieutenant."

"But it is I who have orders from the provincial government, sir." The man looked ugly and determined. "In the name of the governor himself, you are directed to take these distinguished people from Africa aboard your vessel."

Durell murmured, "Let them come on. We don't want a shoot-out with the locals, Agosto."

Agosto nodded and yielded to the police launch. The Lieutenant looked smug. Prince Tim, Sally, and his two seven-foot men came up the gangway. Atimboku grinned. The warrior with the broken wrist now wore a white bandage and a leather strap. The whistle hooted, the local cop saluted, and the great paddlewheels began to churn and thrash at the river current.

"I will take the best suite," Prince Tim announced. "We will not disturb you."

Sally said, "I want to talk to Sam."

"You remain with me. I do not permit it."

Sally was anguished. "Do you understand, Sam? I am his weapon against you. My own brother. He says he will hurt or kill me if you do not cooperate with him." She swallowed. "You remember, he tried to kill me before, when he wanted to gain power in Pakuru. He will do what he threatens to do."

"I remember," Durell said.

Atimboku looked complacent. Agosto ordered a crewman to show them to the cabins aft, and Durell turned away to walk into Inocenza's cabin.

## 2

"Who is she?" Inocenza asked angrily.

"An old friend." He closed the stateroom door. It was oppressively hot in her plush, Victorian cabin. "How is O'Hara?"

"He complains of piracy. He says strange things, but I do not understand them. How good an old friend, Sam?"

"I helped Sally a few years ago."

"She is very beautiful, but she is African. I have American blood in me, O'Hara says."

"Forget Sally. Just what is O'Hara mumbling about?"

"You, mostly. He fears you. How can I forget a beautiful woman you once loved? Why is she with us?"

"There is nothing to be jealous about, Inocenza."

"Jealous?" She pretended to be offended. Her big hoop earrings shone as she tossed her head. "She is nothing to me. You will come to know me, Sam. We will travel together to wherever you want to go."

"I wish I knew where that was."

"But I know the place," Inocenza said. "Of course, I know the place."

He looked at her sharply. "You do?"

"You never asked *me*, Sam. Ask me now." She put her hands on her hips. "Ask me properly."

"Don't be a bitch," he said.

"But you have not been nice to me."

"What is O'Hara saying about me?"

"Ask me where it is you want to go, Sam."

She stood in the doorway, blocking his path. O'Hara sprawled on the bed. Underfoot, the deck trembled as the old engines struggled against the river's hard current. O'Hara made a groaning sound. His bald head gleamed in the light. The curtains were drawn across the cabin windows, the small fan whirred, and O'Hara's sweat permeated the stifling air. Durell pushed past the standing girl and said over his shoulder, "I thought you said you wanted him dead. But you're taking good care of him now."

"He is only a frightened old man, now."

"What is he frightened of?"

"You, Senhor Sam."

He looked down at O'Hara on the rumpled bed. The old man wasn't faking. His bearded face was covered with cold sweat. Spittle drooled down one side of his chin. He had not been injured; and it was not just his drinking. A riverman like O'Hara would have to be in a deep trauma to ignore the movement of his vessel, even through a drunken stupor.

"O'Hara?"

"Lemme 'lone."

"O'Hara, where do we go from Tiparucu, upriver?"

"It's end of the line. Railroad there."

"The railroad is long gone, O'Hara."

"With lots of good men. Death's Railroad, they called it. Finneran, O'Malley, Gadsby—all good men. Dixieland. Good Confederates. Fever got 'em. Bugs. Dysentery. Heat. Jaguar got Tommy Lee. Stupid boy. Good times, though. All dead and buried out there. All in the forest, dead and buried."

"Look at me, O'Hara. Come back from the past."

All at once the fat *capitão* opened his eyes. He glared up at Durell's tall figure, outlined against the light of the pink lamp. His mouth opened and he tried to spit up at Durell and only succeeded in wetting his matted beard.

"Goddam you to everlasting hell, Jonathan! I did what I did, and it was long ago, and you oughta forget it now—"

"What did you do, long ago?" Durell asked quietly.

"You upright, lucky bastard, you 'n' Clarissa, and me workin' for you on the *Trois Belles!* But I got smarter than you, hey? I made a deal with Don Federico, down in Brazil, hey? To hell with your contract. So what if I jumped ship?"

"O'Hara," Durell said. "O'Hara, I'm not Jonathan. He's my grandfather."

"He sent you to kill me, didn't he? He did! He ain't forgot a thing, the old varmint, the luckiest damned card man on the Mississippi." A ghastly chuckle came from O'Hara's wet, open mouth as he glared at Durell. All at once he sat up, fat arms bracing his weight on the bed. His eyes looked blind. "I did nothin' wrong, you hear? I never meant to hurt Jonathan. I tried to send her—I told her to go back to you—"

"Who?" Durell asked quietly. He felt cold, despite the heat in the cabin. "Are you talking about my grandmother? She died in Bayou Peche Rouge a long time ago. Before I was born. When you couldn't have been more than in your early twenties."

"Clarissa was a real lady, a real pretty gal, you know

that?" O'Hara gasped. "So what are you, a ghost come to haunt me? I need 'nother drink." The fat man collapsed backward on the bed. Great tears welled in his rheumy eyes. "Wasn't my fault. Not my fault at all. You lemme alone, you hear? Why'd you come here after all these years? Why? You oughta feel sorry for me, a sick, fat old man. . . ."

Durell looked at Inocenza. Her face was stricken; she was oddly subdued. "Did he ever talk like this before?"

"No. Never."

"Do you know what he's talking about?"

"No, I swear it. Why do you look like that? What is the matter with you, Sam? He thought you were someone else, yes? A someone from his past."

"I suppose so. Inocenza, where do we go from the river-town upstream? You do know, don't you?"

"Why, he just told you. The old place. It is far back in the forest from Tiparucu. I do not understand, because no one goes there now. It was Don Federico's old rubber plantation, fifty, maybe seventy years ago. He told me all about Don Federico, who bought O'Hara and this boat so long ago. But the rubber men are all dead now, Sam. The whole forest is dead. It is filled with the ghosts of all the Indians who died tapping the trees, and the young Americans who came here to make their fortune and died of disease in the jungle. He named them all. You heard him. But there are nothing but graves there, Sam."

"Don Federico's old plantation," he repeated.

"*Sim.*"

## 3

*O Rio Xapajos* was desolate and uninhabited beyond a few satellite villages near Paramaguito. After that was the forest, dark and gloomy under the brassy equatorial sun, heavy with foliage, the trees unmoving with no wind to stir them. Manoel followed the west bank channel with extreme care. Driftwood, a few dead animals, an overturned Indian canoe were all that broke the swift red current of the river. The distant shore was only a smudge seen through the heat haze and humidity. Now and then a fish broke the surface with a mighty splash, startled by the churning paddlewheels and the chuffing twin stacks high above the pilot house. If there were people in this shadowed forest, they kept out of sight.

It was a long, hot day. They took turns keeping watch in the pilothouse, and Durell snatched some sleep in one of the staterooms on the upper deck. Nothing changed during the long hours of the afternoon. The river seemed limitless. O'Hara kept to his stateroom, although Durell refused him any more liquor. Later, he went down and talked to the fat man, who was eating a plate of beans that Inocenza had fixed for him. His eating habits were as slovenly as his appearance.

"Don Federico?" O'Hara muttered through a mouthful of food. His eyes were sober and sly now. "A perfectly grand man, the last of the great gentlemen. He knew how to live, my boy, in the high manner. Everything he wanted, he got, ordering from the States sometimes, but mostly from Europe. Nothing but the best. Grand piano, crystal chandeliers, fine silver, carpets from Persia—the finest, the very best. A grand man. When he wanted a riverboat, he bought the *Duos Irmãos* and put it on this here river. The rail terminal came down to Tiparucu, see. He built the railroad from his rubber trees to the river, and I took the smoked balls down to Paramaguito, sometimes all the way to Belém. Made a fortune, he did."

"How many men died on the railroad?"

O'Hara looked at him with piggish eyes. "Nobody counted, in them days. It was like the Alaska goldrush, only everybody was after a rubber stake then. Get rich quick by roundin' up a Indian tribe and makin' 'em work, even if you had to stick guns in their ribs and hold their women on the plantation. The bastards wouldn't work too good, though. Died like flies. Just sickened and died. Nobody counted, like I say."

"What happened to Don Federico?"

"Well, the bubble broke finally when the Asians broke the Brazilian monopoly. Don Federico was a gentleman, sonny. He knew how to cut his losses. He would've made a fine riverman on the Mississippi, in the old days. He didn't even count his losses; he just up and quit, packed up and went back to Lisboa. Died a few years ago, I hear, at the age of ninety-two. Big Society funeral, respected man, all that. A real gentleman. Gave me the *Duos Irmãos* before he left for Portugal. A long time ago, sonny. I disremember the details. Slim pickings for years, like a blight hit the whole river territory. Then I built up a bit of steady trade, a scheduled passenger run, and I did pretty good; but it's always nip and tuck."

O'Hara paused and belched. "You look here, young Durell. I'm a man for hire, see? You need my help, an' if you pay more than the folks at the old plantation right now, I'm yours. Me and the ship."

"Who are the folks at the plantation?"

"Nobody really knows. I only seen the flunkies."

"You must have some idea," Durell insisted.

O'Hara ran sausage fingers through his beard. "I been honest with you, sonny."

"Not honest enough."

O'Hara looked aggrieved. "Inocenza tells me I talked a lot when I was sick this morning. Nothing to it. I get dreams, like. Don't mean nothing."

"You mentioned my grandmother, Clarissa Durell."

"Yeah. Well, she was a right smart lickety-split gal. Pretty as an old chromo. Crazy about your grandpappy. Lovely woman. I was only a kid when I last saw her."

"How did she die?" Durell asked.

"Lordy, boy, how would I know? I come down here with the *Duos Irmãos* and worked for Don Federico. Didn't hear about her unfortunate passing until years later. Unfortunate, 'cause she was so young. Gave birth to your daddy, who was killed in an auto accident with your ma, I heard, too."

"Yes. How do you get to Don Federico's station from Tiparucu?"

"Can't rightly say. It's been a long time. There was kind of a road there, up from Paramaguito along this river, but it's broken down and got lots of fallen trees, I reckon. Need a Jeep. River traffic's easier."

Durell said tightly, "You didn't mention the road before."

"Why bother? Nobody uses it. The river is quickest."

During the late afternoon, the estuary of the Rio Xapajos began to narrow. The opposite bank became distinct, marked by endless forests. They had stopped once at a small landing on their side of the river to pick up cordwood as fuel for the steamboat's engines. Nobody was near the small shack beside the river's bank. A caiman dozed in the mud and the sun. Durell stepped ashore, after ordering Wells and Agosto to stay in the pilothouse. Insects whirred, hummed, chewed and bit at him. The small dock was treacherous with broken planks. The caiman lifted his alligatorlike head and stared at him. He looked at the rutted trail that ran from the shack into the dark gloom of the trees. Parrots squawked and flashed among the leaves. He could see no junction from the trail that led inland from the road O'Hara had described to Tiparucu, but a broken-down old Chevrolet truck, painted bright yellow with Indian decorations in red stood beside the shack. The truck was empty. He went into the shack, kicking open the plank door.

The floor was dirt, the furnishings a hammock and a camp stove. The river glittered through cracks in the planked siding. A man lay in the hammock, his bare legs and arms dangling. There was a small pool of dark blood on the floor. Ants were busy at it, a squirming black blot against the sand. The heat inside was like an oven, but there was no smell yet.

The man had been shot in the back of the neck. The face was just a face, coffee-colored, with surprised eyes.

He went outside and studied the trail. There were tire marks in the dirt; they did not match the tires on the broken-down truck. An axe glittered in the stump of a nearby tree. Cordwood was stacked a short distance from the landing.

He went back to the boat and climbed aboard. Inocenza

was waiting at the gangplank. "What is it, Sam? You have that strange expression on your face again."

"It's nothing."

"Come with me to my cabin. It is two more hours to São Felice. A small junction. You should rest, Sam."

He shook his head and went up to the pilothouse. He said nothing about the dead man at the fueling station.

## 4

"São Felice," Manoel said. "And the Devil's Falls."

"Can we go around it?"

"*Sim*," said Manoel.

"No," said O'Hara.

Durell looked at the two men. "Which is it?"

Manoel flushed under his dark skin. "The river conditions are bad. It is a narrow channel. It has been done, senhor, but not for some years, not in the *Duos Irmãos*."

O'Hara said rustily, "It's the end of the trip. São Felice, and there she is, a stinkin' hole."

The river town was only a collection of thatched huts, a stone church with a domed belfry, a single dock like a broken skeletal finger thrust into the stream. The river was definitely narrower here, and a reddish foam marred its formerly smooth surface. A dull, endless roaring came from around a bend upstream. Durell suppressed his anger. Neither man had mentioned the falls. It was not even marked on the sketchy pilot's chart he had studied. There was a vague indication of a second narrow river channel, but he had to take O'Hara's word for it.

"Willie?"

Wells sat in the back of the pilothouse. "Yo, Sam."

"How much explosives did you dig up aboard?"

"Enough to blow us all up over the halls."

O'Hara said, "What are you talking about? It's my dynamite. You can't have it—"

Durell ignored him. The town seemed peculiarly empty. He knew that the *Duos Irmãos* made this trip once every five or six weeks, and their arrival should have stirred up some commotion on the waterfront. From the domed church came the mournful tolling of an iron bell. A long open shed with a sagging tin roof paralleled the old dock. The sun in the west made an impossible glare behind the town. Manoel pulled the engine-room signal and the heavy clank of the rocker arm slowed and the big paddles halted as they drifted toward the landing.

Wells stared at the shore and said, "I don't like it."

Durell felt the shaking vibration of the deck as the paddlewheels were reversed to check their momentum. "The channel is out. I think O'Hara is right. Better get Agosto."

"I wish Belmont was here."

Durell said nothing to that. There was a small fleet of fishing canoes on the red sand beach, but no Indians were present, and in the clearing beyond, where slanted stalls of palm-thatched roofs were scattered, no children played, no women did marketing. At this time of day, the men who worked the river's teeming fishbeds should have been hauling in their catch—

"Manoel," he said sharply. "Sheer off."

When the pilot hesitated, Durell seized the big wheel and spun it savagely to port, hoping to turn the bow off the approaching dock. The reversing paddles helped, but not enough. The steamboat had almost lost way. He felt the push of the river current, made stronger by the falls just around the bend. There was only a foot of freeboard between the main deck and surface of the water. Foam churned from the paddlewheel housings. His left hand shot out to the engine-room signal, but the Indian engineer down there had already shut down, anticipating the landing. The *Duos Irmãos* drifted helplessly toward the broken-down dock.

The stutter of an automatic rifle stitched through the heat of the afternoon air. Glass broke and flew wickedly from the shattered pilothouse windows. O'Hara gave out a thunderous curse and threw himself on the deck behind the wheel. Durell turned to Willie Wells.

"Use the dynamite, Willie."

O'Hara yelled, "Hey, wait—my boat—"

More rifles opened up. Wood splinters whistled through the air. More glass crashed. Durell ducked from the narrow door and ran around the pilot house to where he could see the dock. Men had come out of its black shadows, all armed, and ran down the pier. The steamboat hit the first pilings with a shudder that knocked Durell from his feet. He was up again, crouching, in a moment. Willie Wells slid down the ladder to the hurricane deck, his feet not touching the treads, and a bullet slammed into a post near him as he ducked out of sight.

The boat crashed helplessly against the dock, splintering planks in a shower of broken, flying timbers. More than a dozen armed men came running to board the vessel while others appeared from the shacks and sheds along the beach. The *Duos Irmãos* shuddered to a stop.

Someone, perhaps Manoel, pulled the ship's whistle and its piercing blast overwhelmed the quick rattle of automatic rifle fire. Durell did not fire in return. There were really two groups of attackers, he saw. One group of men were Western-dressed Europeans. Russians, he guessed. The other group, coming toward the bow, were Chinese, wearing slacks and dark shirts and sneakers. Each side had appointed flankers to keep a wary eye on the other. Durell yelled up to Manoel to blow the whistle again. At the same time, Willie Wells returned with several sticks of dynamite. Two of the crewmen stuck their heads out and were shot at. The Chinese came over the bow, onto the deck. Four of them. The Russians leaped aboard amidships.

"Vladim Vodaniev!" Durell called.

The tallest Russian paused, his head jerking up to look at Durell's level gun. "Ah. You must be the Cajun. We are taking your ship."

"And your friends from Peking?"

"We are allies—for the moment."

"You don't have a ship to take," Durell said. "In two minutes it will be blown sky-high."

"You bluff, Cajun."

"Try me. You're welcome to stay aboard. Inocenza! O'Hara!"

The firing stopped. The Chinese came cautiously along the main deck, their weapons ready. Agosto appeared, herding Inocenza and O'Hara. The girl looked angry and frightened as she saw the men who had boarded the vessel. She came to Durell and stood beside him, but he did not look at her.

"Agosto, get Prince Tim and Sally. *Depressa!* Quick!"

A muffled explosion came from deep inside the engine room. O'Hara groaned and cursed in Portuguese. There was a smell of fire and oil in the air. The Russian, Vodaniev, took a step backward. "You are speaking truly?"

"Truly," Durell said grimly.

"We will go ashore. You and your people go with us."

The four Chinese looked angry. One of them lifted his rifle at Durell, and another knocked it aside with a quick word. Then the Chinese said, "Mr. Durell, we only wish some transportation. We are all marooned here. We have a common destination, a common purpose, a deadline. Who knows who will win the thing we each want, if we are not there on time?"

"Yes, but you don't go on this boat," Durell said.

Willie Wells came up from the engine hatch and ran down the deck. His face was sweaty. He still held two of the dynamite sticks. One of them, on a long fuse, was sputtering. Durell looked at it calmly.

"Let's dispense with all weapons, shall we?"

## 5

The steamboat burned furiously. There were two more explosions that toppled her twin stacks with tremendous splashes into the river. Flame gouted from her cabins. The black smoke silted the sky. The heat of the fire drove them all from the dock, into the empty town. People appeared, timidly, men and women and children. Dogs barked in the streets. The bell in the dome of the plastered Portuguese church kept tolling.

"Did you get to O'Hara?" Durell asked.

Willie Wells nodded. "I gave him a fresh bottle. He

won't talk to anyone. And Agosto is sticking close to him."

"Good. Then come with me."

Sally stood beside her royal brother, Prince Atimboku, who looked disdainfully at the small knot of Russians under Vodaniev. Farther off, beyond the shed, stood the four Chinese, talking in quiet voices. No need for their weapons now, Durell thought grimly, with the *Duos Irmãos* burning to the waterline. The heat of the late afternoon sun scorched the back of his neck, and he took his sunglasses from his shirt pocket. Vodaniev was the best man the Soviets had—a shrewd agent whose cover as economic commissioner had given him espionage advantages all over Europe and Africa. Vodaniev watched him warily. Prince Tim held Sally by the wrist as she looked toward Durell for help. Atimboku dragged her up the main street of São Felice and loudly began to demand a truck from a frightened man in dirty white pants and a straw hat. The man simply stared at the burning steamboat, his mouth open. A last explosion made a thick gout of flame and smoke gush from the hurricane deck. Durell watched the vessel burn with curious emotions. She had been the sister ship of the vessel in Bayou Peche Rouge where he had been brought up, where old Grandpa Jonathan still lived. He felt a nostalgia and a sense of guilt, which he quickly shook off as Vladim Vodaniev approached him.

"*Gospodin* Durell." The Russian's broad face smiled, full of wrinkles and creases. "It is an ironical situation, *nyet?* You and I—and the rich African imperialist potentate—and Mr. Soo Piao Kim, a gentleman from the Blue Lotus, Peking's military intelligence—always at odds with the Black House in Peking, eh? We all have the same objective. We must have a truce now. You have efficiently stranded us all here by destroying the vessel. We had intended, of course, to reach the auction without you. Now we must decide how to go on."

"How can you decide," Durell said, "when you don't know the final destination?"

The Russian hesitated, shrugged chunky shoulders, and looked at Mr. Soo, the Chinese. "We must be honest with each other. Do you know where the next directive was to take us?"

"I do. And I'm the only one who knows," Durell said.

Willie Wells came up behind him, standing a bit to his left where his drawn gun was aimed at Vodaniev's stomach. There was a watchful waiting from Mr. Soo and his Chinese. Up the street, Atimboku still raged at the local man, demanding a vehicle, and then the African prince took off with a long stride toward the church. The bell had stopped tolling. Chickens scattered from Atimboku's path as he dragged Sally with him.

Durell said, "I agree we must have a truce. Get rid of your arms, and I'll take you where we all want to go."

"But it is you who must cooperate!"

"Do you think your weapons will force me to talk?"

Mr. Soo approached, wincing at the heat that billowed at them from the burning ship. "I believe Mr. Durell is correct. After all, we are on a legitimate mission, all of us."

"But there's an illegal group from the Black House, somewhere about," Durell said. "And an Albanian, named Stepanic."

"Yes, we know." The Chinese was impassive. "Did you mean it, sir, when you said you know our destination? How did you get such information?"

"Does it matter?" Durell's manner was cold. These were top men, brilliant and dedicated to the business. It was inevitable on this job that their trails would cross. They were not rogue groups, like Stepanic's, or half-mad with a lust to get the formula, like Atimboku. He glimpsed Inocenza helping two crewmen carry O'Hara into the shade of the shed by the river. A flock of brilliant forest birds suddenly flew like a rainbow across the hot sky. O'Hara was singing in a raucous voice. His beard bristled as he threw back his head and bellowed his bawdy verses. Inocenza's concern for O'Hara puzzled him. He turned back to Vodaniev and Mr. Soo.

"We can all go together if you put down your arms. I won't help you with a gun in my back. Otherwise, you're welcome to try the forest trails yourselves. You won't get far."

He had only Willie Wells to support him, and everything hung in the balance. These others outnumbered him three to one. He felt a cold sweat on the nape of his neck as he met Mr. Soo's bland eyes. It would mean nothing to either the Chinese or the Russian if they killed him. He had to break the impasse quickly.

He said, "Willie, there seems to be a kind of general store over there." He pointed to the hot, dusty plaza of São Felice, where the brown church stood. "Pick up some blankets, hammocks, axes. Throw your gun in the river first. Take mine, too."

"Sam—"

"Do as I say. Tell Agosto to get rid of his, also."

The black man shrugged. "You're the boss, Cajun."

Mr. Soo said mildly, "Do you plan to *walk* from here?"

"It may take three days. There are no roads now. Prince Atimboku is looking for a vehicle that will only prove useless." He watched Wells throw their guns in the river. "Gentlemen?"

Vodaniev said, "You will lead us, then?"

"Only if you get rid of your weapons."

At that moment, he saw Belmont coming down the dusty street of São Felice.

## 6

The tall, cadaverous man was alone. He wore a ragged straw hat, white trousers hitched up with a length of rope, and sandals; he dragged along an unwilling goat with another piece of rope. His shirttails were dirty, flapping around his waist. There was a yellow cloth tied around his throat as a neck band. He looked tired, slow-moving, as he turned to curse at the goat in Portuguese. When he looked up briefly, under the wide brim of his straw hat, he gave no hint of recognition. Durell did no more than glance at him, but Willie Wells stirred.

"We will need someone as a guide," Durell said.

Vodaniev said, "You claim you know the way."

"I said I know our destination. It will not be easy to

reach through the forests. One day's journey could lose us all, going around in circles."

The Russians and the Chinese conferred again. Belmont settled himself fifty yards away, in the shade of the big shed, tethering the goat. If Belmont was still armed, it could prove the ultimate ace in the hole. Not that he expected the others to totally disarm themselves, either.

Wells came back with three men from São Felice, carrying bundles that contained hammocks, extra boots, packs of food, and indeterminate supplies. A decision was suddenly made.

"Very well," Vodaniev said. "We will all go together. Mr. Soo?"

"Yes."

At that moment a frustrated Atimboku came down the main street with his two men guarding an angry, frightened Sally.

Durell looked into the girl's pleading eyes.

"We'll take them, too," he said.

Mr. Soo said gently, "Oh, but that is not necessary."

"We'll take everyone," Durell insisted. "And a guide. I'll talk to that man over there, with the goat."

He walked toward Belmont.

## Chapter Eight

DURELL knelt beside O'Hara, near the feeble little smudge fire that each party had made for itself. The night was filled with shrilling, chirping, humming insects.

"We should have left him in São Felice," he said.

Inocenza looked up. "He'll get better. He is a very hard —very tough—old man."

"Not that tough. He can't walk much farther."

"He will rest tonight. Tomorrow he will be better. No more liquor for him, please."

He looked at the girl curiously. "I thought you hated him, Inocenza."

"I do. But can one leave him to die? You destroyed his boat. It was his livelihood. It was all he had. I think he maybe died with it. He loved the *Duos Irmãos* like he never loved me—or any other woman." She studied Durell's shadowed figure in the dim firelight. "Besides, he truly knows the way, whatever you told those others." She gestured with contempt toward the Russians, Chinese, and Atimboku. "They know nothing. Neither do you. It is O'Hara who can take you to Don Federico's."

"Have you ever been there?"

"No. But O'Hara talked much of it. The best time of his life was when he worked for Don Federico."

"Has he been back there lately?"

She pushed back her thick hair. "One month ago, I think. I was glad to be rid of him for a few days. Manoel and I, we ran the ship. It was a beautiful ship, in its way."

"What did O'Hara say when he got back?"

"*Nehouma cousa,*" she said. "Not a thing. But he was happy. He had a lot of money. He bought me the gold chain and crucifix." She touched herself between her breasts and looked up at him ruefully. "It was the only real present he ever gave to me, you understand."

Durell looked down at the exhausted fat man. The liquor had kept O'Hara going during the first leg of the trail out of São Felice. For a time, the villagers had followed their curious safari, but then one by one, as they passed into the gloom of forest and swamp beyond the falls, they had dropped away, crossing themselves. O'Hara had kept up his drunken singing until nightfall, and they had walked only by the light of a swollen, ochre moon. Then he had gone silent except for his panting and grumbling. Two hours later he needed to be helped, and Willie Wells stayed constantly at his side, keeping him from Vodaniev and Mr. Soo. Now Durell listened to the old man's breathing and felt a touch of worry.

"O'Hara?"

"Go to hell, sonny," O'Hara whispered. "Unless you can get another drink for me."

"There isn't another bottle with us. You said there was an old railroad bed we could follow," Durell persisted.

"That's right. Up at the river fork."

"How far is it from here?"

"I dunno. Where are we now? Near the river?"

"Yes, about twenty miles south of São Felice."

"Tomorrow morning, then. We hit it tomorrow. Now lemme alone," O'Hara grunted. "Lemme sleep. Inocenza, come on, bed down with me, be a good girl."

The girl sat down on the leafy forest floor beside the old man and held his hand.

Wells said quietly, "Better get some sleep, Cajun. I'll stand watch. You talked to Belmont yet?"

"I will, when it looks all right."

"He appears to have been through the wringer."

"He'll tell us all about it."

Wells hesitated. Durell sat down on the spongy forest floor and leaned back against a tree. The campfires of the Chinese and the Russians were flickering down. Clouds began to obscure the big moon. He hoped it wasn't going to rain. Then Wells said, "What do you make of O'Hara?"

"He hasn't told us all he knows."

"About this Don Federico's place?"

"About me. About Grandpa Jonathan."

Wells said, "I can't figure that Inocenza. Given another time and place, I'd go for that jungle kitten."

"Just keep your eye on Prince Tim's little group of murderers, Willie."

"You bet."

**2**

Belmont lay in a tattered hammock strung between two small trees away from the campfire. He had thrown a mosquito netting over his face. The smell of swamp water pervaded the night. A wind had begun to stir in the high treetops, bringing with it the distant sound of the river.

"That Mr. Soo," Belmont said. "I think he's on to me. He came over and started asking questions. Very polite Chinese gentleman. He wanted to know about my wife and family and São Felice, how often I came into the forest, did I know of any special places of interest in the area. I pretended I couldn't understand half of what he said. Used pidgin English on him, some rough Portuguese, a bit of Tupamaca dialect."

"Where did you learn Tupamaca?" Durell asked.

"It's all in my files. I once worked this area—well, not exactly here, but farther along the river, at Manaus. That time we had our consul snatched by terrorists and held for ransom, back in '69."

"What about Stepanic? You didn't catch up with him?"

"No. And I don't think Stepanic shafted Andy."

"Why not?"

"It's a feeling I have, that's all."

"Any candidates to take Stepanic's place?"

Belmont lifted himself a bit in his hammock and looked at the glowing smudge fires of the other groups. Somewhere in the forest, someone or something coughed. One of the Russians got up and took a few steps into the bushes to relieve himself. Belmont waved a hand. "Take your pick, Cajun. I don't know why Andy's killing gravels me so much."

"It bothers me, too."

"I mean, why pick him out? It doesn't smell right. Have you been thinking about it?"

"All the way. Take it easy, Belmont. Where do you figure Stepanic is now?"

"Somewhere ahead of us. He came as far as São Felice. That was yesterday morning. Then he hiked out this way with his two Chinese rogue goons from the Black House. I had a good talk with the priest at São Felice. Friendly feller, from Rio, originally. He said two small planes flew over this area early yesterday morning, which would be about the time we were at Paramaguito. Private planes. He didn't think they were from the mineral surveyors, the Companhia Meridional. Didn't look like the ones they usually use. But he couldn't identify them."

"All right."

"You want me to take a watch?"

"Agosto will stand by, after Willie's trick."

"Good. I could use the sleep."

"Belmont," Durell said, "don't go off half-cocked again."

"You're the boss, Cajun."

The hammock was soft and comfortable. Sleep tugged at all his senses. Even the insects were no longer a torment, now that the wind moved through the Amazon forest. He listened to the night birds, the sound of branches creaking, the distant rumble of the river. He thought of the *Duos Irmãos,* still regretting having had to destroy it; but it had been necessary to keep everything in balance. He could not have allowed Mr. Soo or Vodaniev to strand him in São Felice.

Someone crept up to the head of his hammock.

He did not move or betray his awareness. He had no weapon, only his hands. He lay still, nerves suddenly tingling, his muscles ready to bunch and spring.

"Sam?"

It was Sally Hukkim.

"Come in," he whispered.

She stood where he could dimly see her face in the fitful light of the clouded moon. The wind made a branch fall somewhere in the swampy forest nearby. Sally's dark face was in the shadows. Her fine nose and arched brows were highlighted, and he saw that she had tied up her long, silken hair in a knot at the nape of her neck, to relieve herself from the heat. She reached out and touched him.

"May I?"

"Come in," he repeated. "How did you get away from Atimboku?"

"My royal, murdering brother thinks it's safe for me now. I have no place to go, out here in the forest. He knows I have to stay with him now."

"Stay with me," he suggested.

She slid gently into the hammock with him. Her body was warm and soft, pliant against him. He remembered their two weeks in Mozambique so long ago. She had gone back then to Pakuru, to assume her royal duties when the old Queen Elephant, her mother, had suddenly died. He remembered the turquoise look of the Indian Ocean, the bending coconut palms, the hotel cottage they had shared.

"Has Atimboku threatened you again?" he whispered.

"Only to make you take him along."

"Would he really hurt you?"

"He tried to kill me once, you remember; when he thought I stood in his way to power in Pakuru. He's much worse now. Almost paranoid. The country lives under his constant threat of terror; he's a tyrant, Sam. And now that Pakuru is rich, he will not be stopped from anything he wants. Yes, he would hurt me, kill me if necessary, to make you cooperate."

"He wants the Zero Formula that badly?"

"He'd sell our whole country, mortgage it forever, to get it. He is so hungry for power, he's a bit mad."

Durell sighed and held her closer. "Stay with him for a little while longer, please."

"Yes, if I must. But Sam—do you remember the times when you and I—"

"I remember."

She somehow managed to smell fresh and clean here in the Amazon's swampy forests. The moon came out briefly and he saw her luminous golden eyes, her face close to his in the broad striped hammock. He reached for her and kissed her lightly. Her mouth reacted hungrily to his. The forest around them suddenly seemed to go silent. She wore nothing under her loose Pakuran skirt and blouse.

"Sam?" she whispered.

"Hush."

"Sam, for two years I thought of you—wondered if I had made a mistake to go back to my country—"

"You did the right thing."

"I know, but—"

"Hush," he said again.

The hammock was very comfortable for the two of them.

## Chapter Nine

THE insects forced them up before dawn. There was no sun. Gray clouds tumbled overhead, seen through the high umbrella of trees branching overhead. Belmont was up, his hammock already packed. Sally had slipped away and returned to her brother's little camp. The Chinese were the last to get themselves ready for the trek. Belmont, in his tattered, wide-brimmed straw hat and gaunt, bronzed face looked the part of a halfbreed guide, wearing his loose white jacket and floppy trousers supported by the length of rope.

O'Hara seemed better. Inocenza made some coffee for them all, watching Durell with curiously bitter eyes. When he drank the steaming liquid in the vaporous gray dawn, she spoke in a voice like a spitting jungle cat.

"Was she that good?"

"We're old friends, Inocenza."

"Ha! Because my Portuguese skin, always in the sun, is a bit darker than her Chinese and black and whatever-it-is her mother had—is that why you—"

"Nothing like that."

"I saw you first, I offered you anything you wished—but you did not find me desirable, is that it?"

"No, that's not it," he said patiently.

"Was she good? You made to love for a long time, eh? I was not asleep. I saw her sneak to you, the African bitch. Who does she think she is? She is no better than I! I know how to love a man—"

"Please help O'Hara get started," he said.

Willie Wells had picked up a compass in São Felice, along with other supplies. They began walking southwest, after Belmont spoke to the bleary-eyed O'Hara. There were no trails in the endless gray forest to show where they were going. The ground was squashy underfoot, and twice before nine o'clock they had to wade through hip-deep bogs and over swampy islets in a colorless miasma that seemed to go on forever. The sky, the forest, the trees were all gray. They were like ghosts struggling through an eternal mist. It soon became a desperate, despairing business. They stumbled, tripped and fell, got up to climb over massive windfalls of huge, half-rotted logs, then bogged down again in the squashy, quaky forest floor. Within the hour after they started, it began to rain, a warm wet drizzle that soon soaked them all to the skin, compounding their misery. They panted, cursed, and struggled forward. In the swampy areas, Agosto and Belmont went ahead to beat the water with branches to frighten off snakes. They could not see the sky through the overhanging branches of the tall trees, and soon few of them had the strength or inclination to look forward beyond their next footstep.

Insects were another plague added to the mud. Clouds of them in all shapes and sizes descended on them, crawling into their shirts and up their trousers, biting and stinging, fighting to get into their mouths and eyes. Few of them were familiar, and the size of the largest was appalling. There seemed to be no escape from them. One of the Russians, stung more virulently than the others, suddenly screamed and flung himself face down into a thick puddle of mud and water, thrashing about and plastering his face with the mud in an effort to ease the torment.

Orchids hung from the gray tree branches, and now and then a mass of brightly colored birds flocked around them as they pushed on desperately. The beauty of the birds and the tropical foliage belied the primeval dangers of their trek. No one spoke to his neighbor. Wading knee-deep through the mud to the next relatively high area of the forest floor, Inocenza clung desperately to Willie Wells, and Sally, trying to go on with solemn fortitude, suddenly moaned and fell to her knees.

"Sam! Sam!"

He turned back to her. The warm, sullen rain, that sometimes came in bursts like a waterfall, streamed down her face, plastered her thick black hair to her head, made her torn clothing cling to every rich curve of her body. Durell helped her to her feet, noting that Prince Atimboku and his bodyguard ignored her.

"You have to go on," he said gently.

"I know, but—"

"Come on," he urged her.

The others trudged past without looking at them. Sally looked at the Chinese and the Russians with bitter eyes. "What kind of people are they?" she whispered. "What kind of a man are you, Sam? I know they have orders, but must they be inhuman? This awful place—"

"Hush," he said. "I'll help you."

She clung heavily to him, and slowly he got her to walk again. There was some relief from the insects when the rain grew heavier, but the absence of that evil was more than lost because of the increased slipperiness of the mud and water through which they slogged. Once, he heard a wild pig grunt, and he looked up to see the beast facing them, the tusks gleaming, the tiny eyes red and cruel. Its shaggy body was enormous. Everyone came to a halt, hesitating to display any weapons he should have discarded for the "truce." Durell pushed Sally behind him, and for a moment there was no sound except the distant chittering of monkeys and the hiss and thunder of the rain. But then the great beast suddenly changed its mind about charging them, snorted twice, and trotted off among the colorless, rain-dripping trees.

Time became meaningless, measured only by each step forward. It was another hour before the exhausted party reached the old railroad bed. It suddenly loomed up through the rain like a solid barrier, the crushed stone of the ballast making a wall ahead of them. Everyone halted, bent as if under the weight of the pounding rain, mud-stained, scratched and beaten by branches and vines as if by whips. Belmont scrambled up the incline and waved a white-clad arm. His straw hat was shapeless, dripping with water. His dark eyes were sunken in his head, cadaverous, too bright.

*"Aqui. Aqui mesmo!"* he croaked. "Here, right here!"

The others scrambled painfully up onto the roadbed with groans of relief. Durell looked to right and left along the gentle curve of the right-of-way. The ties were still in place, but the iron rails had long ago been stripped from the bed. Weeds grew waist-high in the cinders and stones, and vines curled down from trees that had been axed and grown up again. Here and there were other, younger trees that had taken root in the middle of the track. Great brakes of bamboo, thick and flowery, twenty and thirty feet high, grew in the ditches and walled them in. But it was road that could be followed, clear and distinct.

Durell gave O'Hara a hand up the embankment. The old man puffed and his face was waxen under his weathered skin.

"Ain't been here for thirty, forty years," O'Hara grunted. His beard dripped rain. "Hell of a place. Full of ghosts. We were all boys then, full of piss and vinegar. Lots of 'em dead and gone now. Good Southern boys, some of 'em kin to the finest Confederate families." The old man managed a lopsided grin. "Their pappys and granddaddies come here after the Civil War and left their kids all over the place, amongst the Indians and locals."

"Which way?" Durell asked.

O'Hara squinted at the wet, sullen sky. "To the right, I reckon. We go south some more."

"Just keep your mouth shut to the others, all right?"

"How much do you pay me for that, sonny?"

"The government will decide about that. We'll double what you received from the people at Don Federico's."

"Ain't enough. They'll likely kill me."

"We'll talk about it later. Are you all right?"

"Inocenza is with me," the old man said.

The others, the four Chinese and the Russian, Vladim Vodaniev, with Atimboku, Sally, and their two warriors, scrambled up the embankment. At that moment, as if on signal, the skies opened and the rain became a thunderous, torrential downpour. It spit, hissed, poured, and hammered at them like a waterfall. It came without warning and did not let up. The curtains of water were blinding and suffocating.

"It's what the Indians called a *pacatu*," O'Hara yelled. "We gotta get out of here."

"We walk," Durell said. "We're late enough as it is."

The others huddled inward on themselves as if for shelter. Durell started off down the old rail embankment. If not for the solid ballast underfoot, they would all have been mired down in mud and streaming water. Belmont moved in beside him as they trudged into the walls of rain. His lips moved, but Durell could not hear him. Then Belmont pretended to slip and went down on all fours, and as Durell knelt to help him up, Belmont spoke in his ear.

"I've got an extra gun. A Browning. Take it."

"Good." Durell slid the heavy weapon into his waistband and took Belmont's arm. "You look sick."

"I'm okay. I've got an old map, too. There's just one stop between São Felice and the plantation. A place called Dixie, can you beat that? Maybe a ghost town, because the Indians say it's cursed and nobody lives in this area now."

Durell squeezed Belmont's arm. "How far?"

"Maybe six or seven miles, I think."

The Russian, Vodaniev, came up, his squat figure hunched against the thundering rain. Mr. Soo loomed behind him. "What is it?" Vodaniev asked.

"The guide slipped and hurt his leg. He says he doesn't want to go on, anyway."

"Why not?"

"He says this whole place is haunted."

"We must go on," Soo interrupted. "Our time is growing quite limited."

"All right, then."

They marched in a straggling column, each group still keeping to itself. Durell felt better with the cold weight of the Browning against his stomach. Presently he heard footsteps stagger up behind up out of the thundering rain. He turned to see Prince Atimboku. The man's eyes were bloodshot with anger.

"It is outrageous. Must we *walk* like this?"

Durell waved a hand. "It would be a long wait if you expect a train." He smiled at the furious African. "You can always turn back, Tim."

Atomboku said, "I never liked you. I don't feel I owe you anything for getting me out of Pakuru that time. You were simply doing a job." The tall black man wiped rain from his face with the flat of his palm. His clothing had suffered rips and tears and looked ragged, but he still managed to emanate a sense of royal, unpredictable power. "Your duty now is to buy the Zero Formula, am I right?"

"Correct."

"But I intend to buy it. How much do you want, Durell?"

Durell looked up at the sky. A wind had risen above the treetops and it drove the torrential rain into their faces.

"I'm not for sale," Durell said.

"You name the price," Atimboku insisted.

"You can't buy everything you want, Tim. And of all the things you've set your rotten heart on, the Zero Formula is one of the things you will *not* have."

"You bastard, nothing will stop me, you hear? You won't live to open your mouth for the bid, understand?"

Durell looked at the man's enraged face, the red muddy eyes in a handsome face gone flabby with self-indulgence. "Go back to Sally," he said. "She has more good in her little finger than you have in your whole rotten carcass."

"Sally will not live, either," Atimboku said. "I know you two are plotting against me. But what I do is for the good of my nation, for Pakuru, for my people." Atimboku drew in a deep, shivering breath. "I have given you fair warning."

"Thanks for nothing."


## 2


The rain slackened after two weary, drenching hours. Durell slogged on steadily, comforted by the Browning thrust into his pants. Agosto walked with Belmont, up ahead. Durell dropped back to O'Hara, who had suddenly sat down in the middle of the causeway, holding his fat stomach in both hands. Inocenza knelt beside him, concerned. Vodaniev stood there, too, and looked up at Durell as he walked back.

"Why do we need this degenerate sack of lard?" the Russian demanded. "Why do you insist we take him with us?"

"He knows the country. And I owe him something for blowing up his steamboat."

"We owe him nothing. He knows nothing. He is only a drunken fool. Mr. Soo and I have been discussing some things that trouble us, Comrade Durell. Your guide, for example. He is more American than Brazilian. And this fat old riverman. And his—his daughter."

Inocenza looked at Durell and said, "O'Hara is sick."

"I need a drink," O'Hara mumbled.

"There's nothing to drink," Durell said. "Get up."

"Can't. This place is haunted. I'm scared."

"I know you're scared, but it isn't because of the ghosts. Get on your feet, O'Hara."

The old man rocked on his fat bottom. The rain shone on his bald head and dribbled into his bristly gray beard. He looked slyly this way and that. "I reckon we're near Dixie, huh?"

"It can't be far. Maybe we can shelter there and rest for a time. Let's go."

"You don't have to go through the town," the old man muttered. "I know a short cut. Railroad took a bend, see? Like a loop, cutting across a neck of land made by the river. Save us ten, fifteen miles, at least."

"We can't go through the swamps after this rain," Durell said. "It will be up to our necks."

"It's still easier," O'Hara insisted.

Vodaniev muttered something to Mr. Soo, who nodded and said quietly, his Chinese face suddenly smiling, "If Mr. O'Hara knows a short-cut and we could save time—"

"Look at the swamps." Durell waved an arm. "If you want to swim for five miles, go ahead. We'll stick to the causeway."

The rain had raised the water level of the surrounding flooded Amazon forest at least two or three feet in the past two hours. Foam and debris, broken limbs and rotting logs, moved in an ominous current northward, piling up along one side of the railroad embankment. There were no hummocks in sight. Overhead, through the long straight cut in the forest made by the roadbed, the gray clouds tumbled in oppressive density. The rain had slackened, only to be replaced by the steady rush of water through the swamp on either hand.

The Russian hesitated. "Perhaps you are right, Durell. We will continue. If this fat old man objects, we will leave him here. His—ah—woman seems to want to take care of him."

O'Hara said, "That's right. Lemme alone. I'll stay right here." His words were an incoherent mumble for a moment. "Too many ghosts in Dixie. Ain't nothin' there, anyway. Jungle's took back all the houses, the whole damned town. Too many dead men there."

"Get up, O'Hara, or I'll blow a hole in your gut right now," Durell said.

O'Hara made a gurgling sound. "You got a gun?"

Durell saw Vodaniev stiffen and said calmly, "I think we all have guns. It's past time for us to be kidding each other."

Mr. Soo said, "You have not kept your word, Durell?"

"Have you?"

Inocenza said, "You would not—in cold blood—"

"Yes, I would. I want O'Hara with us."

She began to tug at O'Hara's arm. "Get up, *Capitão*. He is a bloodthirsty animal, like the rest of these crazy men." She glared at Durell. "He will surely kill you as he says, just the way he blew up your poor boat."

O'Hara shrugged and climbed laboriously to his feet. They went on.

**3**

They reached the way-stop with the improbable name of Dixie a few minutes before noon. It was difficult to identify it even at close hand through the drizzling, slackening rain. Too many decades of abandonment to the jungle had almost obliterated it. There had been a small station, a warehouse with a corrugated tin roof, and a few Indian houses and a small stone church. Trees that were now thirty and forty years old grew in what had been the narrow streets, and vines covered everything with a leafy camouflage until the houses were mere mounds, and the collapsed station only a vague outline beside the right-of-way. Monkeys chittered in the dangling vines that grew from a single canted telegraph pole that somehow had remained standing. Only the stone church, covered with foliage even to its small belfry, retained some outline of its original shape.

Mr. Soo said philosophically, "When man leaves, nature hastens to repair the outrage he committed against her."

O'Hara grumbled, "I told you there was nothin' here."

Atimboku strode ahead, holding Sally by the wrist, and shouted into the gray noonday drizzle. "Anybody at home?" Then he laughed, his white teeth gleaming in his wet black face. "The old witch doctors of the Banda people would have had a ball in this place!"

Vodaniev stared stolidly at the ruins, his fine white snap-brim panama a soggy mess atop his round head. His small saddlenose twitched.

"It is foolish. Perhaps we can shelter and eat in the capitalist church."

"We only have a few cans of rations left," Durell said.

O'Hara said eagerly, "Then we better push on."

Durell stared at him. "You're anxious not to stop here, *Capitão*. Why?"

"Oh, it ain't that. It just brings back too many memories, good times and bad, when we was buildin' the railroad."

"We'll look at the church," Durell decided.

The others pushed ahead, clambering through the vines and wreckage of the forlorn, dripping place. Agosto waited beside Durell. He had produced a poncho from somewhere, which protected his fake police colonel's uniform. He still wore it with a natty flair. His middle-aged figure looked as sturdy as a trapeze artist's. His soft brown eyes were mournful.

"I begin to feel much pity for O'Hara, senhor," he said to Durell. "He has terrible *temer*—fear. As if he suffers guilt, somehow."

"See that everybody behaves, Agosto."

"*Sim,* senhor."

"And Agosto?"

"Yes?"

"Have you a weapon?"

"*Sim.*" The Brazilian did not smile.

Most of the church roof had caved in, and the stone floor was cracked and split by weeds and shrubs that grew in the gloomy interior. Ferns and bamboo and creepers reached for the gray sky seen through the broken roof tiles. The interior had long been stripped of all religious articles, and the place smelled as if wild pigs had made their lairs in here for a dozen generations. Great masses of mold grew on the inner stone walls. Willie Wells scouted for some dry twigs and broken timber and started a small fire. Although the air was warm, they all shivered from the long trek through the downpour. O'Hara sat with his back to a wall and his eyes never left Durell. The Russian bodyguards for Vodaniev did not sit down, although their boss huddled over the little flickering fire, his teeth chattering. Atimboku, Sally, and the two warriors kept near the entrance. Once, Sally started up as if to join Durell, but her brother detained her with a tight hand on her wrist. The Chinese explored the interior of the abandoned church with scientific curiosity, as if they had found some artifacts on a distant planet they were exploring. Mr. Soo accepted some cold beans from the last of their cans and ate with polite but finicky distaste.

There was a broken door at the rear of the church, and Durell forced it open against the pressure of the vines that overgrew it. At first he assumed that the back of the church had simply been reclaimed by the jungle. He heard the rushing sound of the flooded river, perhaps a mile to the east. He wondered how far it was to the plantation once owned by Don Federico. They were all late for the auction. It would have begun today, he thought. But it did not trouble him. Without the major bidders, the Russians and the Chinese and himself, he did not think any final sale of the Zero Formula would be consummated. He wondered how many others had already arrived at the plantation. He was working on a hunch, following O'Hara's words, but it might all be a mistake. Perhaps he was following only a loose thread of the spider's web, and not heading for the center at all. Usually, the flies who reached the center of such a web ended up dead, snapped up by the patient trapper. In this jungle wilderness, he wondered if it all hadn't been some kind of macabre joke. But George's Fields, which seemed so far away in Maryland at the moment, had been real enough. Still, someone was amusing himself at the expense of all the others. He guessed that he and those with him had been given the most difficult approach trail of all. A plane, or a helicopter could have landed them here with little trouble, with a bit of preparation. Perhaps it was a test to discover which of them was the fittest.

He stepped through the broken doorway and discovered the old graveyard.

The rain had almost stopped. Through the treetops he saw the clouds tumbling, breaking up. Everything dripped. A sense of wet heat arose from the boggy ground. Monkeys chattered at him from the nearby vines, and a parrot squawked and flashed away on brilliant wings. Small animals moved hurriedly away, startled by the presence of a human after so many decades. Trees and bamboo grew in what had been the cemetery clearing, but here and there he could still see the mossy gleam of headstones.

"Durell!"

It was O'Hara, and there was a desperate fear in the man's voice.

"Durell, come back, goddam you! *He* sent you here, all right. I know it now! You planned to come here all the time, didn't you? Come back!"

The old man's voice echoed from the inside of the

ruined church behind him. Durell moved on outward, following a fragmentary path among the gravestones. In a dozen paces, he was screened by the tumbled church wall and the brush and bamboo brakes. The monkeys overhead still scolded him. He felt a sense of somber sadness as he read the faded names on the stones.

*Riordan, John, age 26. Southby, Riddle J., 22. Randall, Lee Stokes, 25. Jefferson, Amos Claudius, age 18.*

It went on. All young men of Southern names, all Americans, who came here over sixty years ago to make their fortunes in the rubber boom. They had died of yellow fever, malaria, dysentery, beriberi, and Indian attacks out of the gray, dripping forest. The trees wept for the forgotten bones that lay under the mossy headstones. It had truly been a devil's railroad built here, one that had cost hundreds of lives, for the profit of one Don Federico who gained a fabulous fortune out of brutality and greed and exploitation, and who died at a ripe old age, no doubt, in the comfort of a villa outside of Lisbon. Anger was useless now.

*Jackson, Pickett, O'Meara, Slade.*

He paused and looked back. He did not know what had drawn him into this gloomy place, where even the trees wept, where sorrow was etched on every sad vine. He could see only the vague shape of the church belfry behind him. No one had followed him here. He went on, parting the thick, stubborn vines, squeezing between the mossy boles of trees, his boots sinking into the wet forest humus. A snake wriggled slowly out of sight, in no hurry. The monkeys in the trees off to the left had suddenly fallen silent.

*Durell, Clarissa B., Age 27.*

He stopped.

It was a special place in the forgotten cemetery, surrounded by what had been a small iron railing, but which now was only a skeleton of rust supported by the vines that had grown over and around it. He thought he heard O'Hara shouting for him again, but he wasn't sure of anything in that moment, over the rush of shock and anger in his ears.

*Durell, Clarissa B.*
*Age 27*
*Born, Bayou Peche Rouge, La.*
*April 10, 1888*
*Died Here of Fever*

It was his grandmother's grave.

A shaft of sunlight broke fitfully through the ragged clouds. Durell drew a long, soft breath. There was no mistake. It could not be an error. A number of things about *Capitão* Jack O'Hara clicked into place in his mind, like the pieces of a jigsaw puzzle. Perhaps he had known some of it all along, ever since meeting the old man. All through his boyhood he had been led to believe that his grandma Clarissa had died suddenly in Bayou Peche Rouge, Louisiana; that it had happened while Grandpa Jonathan was up the Mississippi, gambling on the *Trois Belles;* that ever afterward, old Jonathan never ran the sidewheeler again because of grief and a sense of guilt that he had not been present when his love died.

Durell stared for a long time at the mossy, tilted headstone in the dripping forest. Apparently something quite different had happened to Clarissa B. Durell, so long ago.

It was something tied up to O'Hara's guilt and fear and hate.

He straightened slowly, everything in him suddenly tingling, pressure sliding along his nerves and muscles. He felt a low-key, tender agony in him, pity and sudden caution, a hunter's abrupt instinct busying all his senses—

The shot made a flat coughing sound through the dripping rainwater, the faraway rush of the river, the sough of the wind in the trees. The stem of a hanging vine suddenly parted only two inches from Durell's head. There was no time to think. His reaction came from total instinct, a product of his years in the business. He dove for the thick wet humus of the forest floor as the second shot snapped at the old headstone of his grandmother and ricocheted, screaming, through a grove of nearby bamboo.

A rifle, he thought.

But no one in the motley collection of hostile parties he had led here was armed with a rifle. He lay flat. He watched and listened. Rain dripped. The monkeys were silent. The forest birds had flown away, bright streaks of red and yellow. No one in the church was aware of the two shots.

He crawled to the left, away from the headstone. A great wall of bamboo had grown up along the edge of the cemetery, some twenty feet away. He needed to get under the cover there. He rolled onto one shoulder and pulled the heavy Browning from his waistband and held it in his left hand. There was no target. He searched the surrounding bush, the glistening wet trees, taking a quadrant at a time, doing it quickly and efficiently. Silence, except for the drip-drip of the trees. He slid forward on his elbows and belly toward the bamboo. A long shaft of sunlight suddenly sliced through the parting clouds, speeding like a searchlight and through the forest gloom. Something glinted briefly, ahead and a bit to the left. It could have been only refraction from a bead of water on a leaf. He did not think so. He moved forward again. He no longer thought about the astonishing fact that his grandmother had died in this remote, desolate place almost seventy years ago. Someone had expected him here, had been waiting in ambush for him. A patient killer, a professional killer, amused by the bitter humor of Durell's situation, taking his time now until he had a perfect target. He had missed the first shot, the setup, only because Durell had straightened up so suddenly from the gravestone. The killer would be more careful now. And more sure of himself.

He tried to picture O'Hara in the role of the ambusher, but it did not fit. He slid between the thick green stems of bamboo and elbowed forward on his stomach. Something snapped sharply to his left. Far off, the monkeys went screaming through the treetops.

Finally, he came to the edge of the crumbled cemetery wall. He stepped over it with caution. The church was now totally hidden behind him. The Browning was heavy in his hand. To the left, he thought. That's where he is. He watched the vines and creepers, the twinkling of tiny orchids, the evanescent sheen of a butterfly's blue and gold wings. There was no glimpse of the man with the rifle. After a dozen more paces, he paused. The forest was silent. Then something tugged at his shirtsleeve and at the same moment he heard the rifle crack again. The sound was flat and spiteful. He ran in a crouch, squeezing between the trees. To the right now. The assailant had made a half-circle before him. A sudden spatter of falling raindrops from a nearby tree made him turn his head. Again the rifle cracked. This time he felt a sudden impact on his left shoulder that spun him dizzily around and down to his knees.

He felt no immediate pain. He began to sweat. The Browning felt futile in his hand. He could be seen, he felt, his every move marked and followed. But he could not see the man with the rifle who stalked him.

Water shimmered a few paces ahead. He found two trees growing close together and squeezed between them for some protection. His shoulder suddenly began to ache and he saw blood on his shirt. His skin burned where the rifle slug had nicked him. He swore softly and began to search the branches above him, instead of the ground level. Maybe the man was up there somewhere. He thought he heard his name being called from somewhere far behind him.

"Sam! Yo, Cajun?"

It was Willie Wells. Brush crackled behind him in the invisible cemetery. He kept his eyes on the lower tree branches. Light and shade, the gleam of rainwater on huge green leaves, the quicksilver trickle of water running down the smooth stem of a vine. Suddenly it was there. The pattern of darkness and brightening sunlight in the foliage suddenly resolved itself into the silhouette of a man, upright, legs spread, feet braced between two vertical tree limbs. The crotch of the trunk was about six feet off the ground. The rifle barrel made a fragile finger of metallic light, pointing at him. Everything happened at once. Durell raised the Browning, pulled the trigger, and saw the thin flicker of muzzle flame spit at him. The Browning clicked futilely. It did not fire. The rifle bullet whipped past his ear, chunked into a tree. Simultaneously, there were other shots and high yells from the churchyard.

"Cajun!"

The man with the rifle slid down from the tree and became just a pattern of shadows among other shadows in the gray gloom. Splashing sounds came as the man waded away through the knee-deep water that covered the forest floor. Durell tried the Browning again. Again, nothing happened.

It was a trap, he thought. Whoever had seen him at the cemetery had known he would stop at Clarissa's grave. It was a miracle that the first shot hadn't blown his head off. He was up against a pro, a careful man who enjoyed his work. He pushed forward, wading into the water that swirled through the forest, carrying the run-off of the rain toward the distant, swollen river. He heard more yelling and a spasm of shooting from the church behind him. He swore softly and kept his eyes on the shadows ahead. The man had vanished, melting into the thick green of the forest. There were no more shots from ahead.

He checked himself, looked back to orient himself. Only a few dozen steps into this maze of trees and vines, and a man could become hopelessly lost. His shoulder throbbed where the bullet had torn his flesh. Blood kept running down his arm.

"Sam? Sam!"

He turned quickly, trusting no one. It was Willie Wells. Belmont was only a step behind the black man.

"Are you all right, Sam? Your arm—"

"It's nothing. What's going on at the church?"

"*Capitão* O'Hara ran away."

"Hell. And Inocenza?"

"I've got her."

Belmont said, "Who sniped at you, Cajun?"

"I never saw him clearly." Durell looked at the thin man's wet pants, soaked above the knees, plastered with mud. "Where have you been, Belmont?"

"Scouting around, trying to help you." Belmont waved a thin impatient arm. "It's all flood water, out there. Willie only told you the half of it, Cajun. Agosto is gone, too."

Durell waved the useless Browning in his hand. "Who gave you this gun for me?"

"Agosto had it."

"I see. You're sure the others—the Russians, the Chinese, maybe Atimboku—they didn't leave the church?"

"They were all inside, until O'Hara made his crazy run for it, bellowing like an old boar."

"And Sally?"

"Still with Prince Tim."

Durell started back to the church, holding his bleeding shoulder.

## 4

Inocenza said, "Hold still, Sam."

Sally said, "I can fix it."

"I will take care of him," Inocenza said angrily. She sneered, "Why don't you go back to your brother, your royal highness?"

Sally turned abruptly away, her head held high. Inocenza's hands were quick and none too gentle with the improvised bandage she had torn from her blouse. As she knelt forward, her firm breasts strained against the thin fabric. She giggled suddenly. "Did you find what the *capitão* did not want you to find?"

"I think so. Yes."

"I never saw him so afraid of anyone before. Not any man. But he was afraid of you, from the start."

"He has good reason to be afraid. And he has a lot of questions to answer."

"O'Hara is gone now," she said. "He ran away up the railroad bed, going south, ahead of us. I think he has gone to the old place, Don Federico's, that he always talks about from the old days. Your friend Agosto went with him."

"With him, or chasing after him?"

"They left together."

"Before or after the shooting?"

"Before," Inocenza said flatly.

"Then who came after me with that rifle?"

"I do not know, truly. Perhaps it was one of your own friends. They are all such strange, hard men. They are not like other men, not like—like Manoel, who seems an innocent babe compared to all of you. Or to these Russians. The Chinese seemed most civilized, do you not agree? But that Atimboku is like a madman."

"Who do you think shot at me, Inocenza?"

"Perhaps your friend Agosto," she said spitefully. She tore the bandage with her strong white teeth, her head bowed, eyes not meeting his. Her black hair was glossy, with two braided strands tied with bits of colored ribbon behind her small ears. "Why did you not take Manoel along with us? Were you jealous of him?"

"We just didn't need him. Why do you say Agosto left here with O'Hara?"

"Well, the two of them were talking very quietly in a corner, and then Agosto stepped out of the church and then O'Hara suddenly yelled, like a nightmare, you know? And then the *capitão* ran." She finished tying the bandage. "There. Your shoulder will be fine, if it does not get infected in this terrible mud and rain."

"Inocenza, was I meant to find that grave?"

"I do not know what you are talking about."

"Who was waiting for me out there, with the rifle?"

"I do not know. Everyone was here except O'Hara and Agosto."

Her eyes were bland and unfathomable, meeting his. Nothing like a woman scorned, he thought grimly. His rejection of her, and the hours he had shared in the hammock with Sally, had changed her passion into something akin to hate. She tried to hide it, but he saw it there behind her dark, solemn eyes.

# Chapter Ten

THEY slogged on for two more hours, following the long curves of the old roadbed, working their way among the trees and vines that sometimes almost obliterated where the railway had been. Water shimmered on either hand below the embankment. The sun came out in full force and hammered at them with implacable fury. Their clothes steamed, and sweat stung their eyes. A sullen exhaustion gripped them all. Hostility became more evident in the grim, dubious faces that followed Durell. Now and then they had to stop and clear the trees and vines that blocked their way. It had to be done by main force, since they had neither axes nor machetes. The work was done resentfully, under Durell's orders. He took time to check the Browning that Agosto had given Belmont for him. The firing pin had recently been removed. Touches of rust and verdigris covered most of the mechanism, but there were bright sharp scratches where the pin had been forced out. The gun had been meant to give him a sense of false security. He watched Belmont, but saw nothing in the man's gaunt face that looked suspicious. It was Agosto, he thought. Again a number of puzzling pieces fell into place in his mind. None of it helped Durell's humor. His sense of anger and outrage grew more intense with each struggling step forward.

The sun and the insects now were murderous. The others in the small safari straggled farther and farther behind, until they took up almost a quarter of a mile between Durell at the head and Atimboku at the rear. The Russians plodded grimly along; the Chinese displayed an impassivity toward their hardships. None of them had eaten since leaving the desolate church. Atimboku's complaints were loud and bitter, drifting up from the tail of their column. Mostly, he swore at Durell for burning the steamboat that could have taken them up the river in comfort.

All of them now openly displayed the weapons they had pretended to abandon during the truce agreement. It was the world of trickery and deceit in microcosm, Durell thought grimly. A macabre jest, to test their capacity to survive in this untamed, menacing Amazon wilderness.

Belmont moved up beside him. His face was gray, his cheeks sunken, his eyes too bright. He murmured, "So you don't think it was Stepanic who fixed Andy Weyer in Belém?"

"Not likely," Durell said.

"Are you thinking about our teammate, Agosto? He sold us out, didn't he?"

"He was never one of us."

"But you accepted him in Belém," Belmont objected.

"It was necessary. Part of the game plan we were supposed to follow."

"You knew it, but didn't do anything about it?" There was a sharp edge of danger in Belmont's voice.

"Take it easy. I think Andy was able to recognize him. Maybe Andy could tell who he really was. So he was wiped. It's only an educated guess, however."

"But Agosto tried to kill you. It makes no sense," Belmont argued. "If he was one of *them,* they need you, they want you to bid for this goddam formula, they want Uncle Sam's taxpayers' money. So why try to kill you?"

"I don't know." Durell took off his sunglasses and stared at the tall man's bitter face. "Andy's death just made room on our team for Agosto. That's plain enough. That Portuguese intelligence man I mentioned long ago—shouldn't call him Portuguese, really, except that was his first passport, issued in Goa—he played tricks like that in Angola and in Mozambique, in Africa. Tested and taunted the guerillas and terrorists. Just to measure their mettle against his. A twisted sense of humor, perhaps. An incredible self-confidence, a sureness for survival. We'll see about that."

"I'm going to kill him," Belmont said, speaking between his teeth.

"That's an oversimplified answer. Save your breath. It's getting hotter, and we're all thirsty and hungry. Maybe getting a bit irrational. Take it easy."

The break came about two hours before sundown. They were moving slower now, concentrating on each forward step. Every movement had become an enormous effort. They no longer tried to swipe away the vicious clouds of flies and mosquitos that attacked them. Several times in the last few minutes, Inocenza staggered and fell, and it was always Willie Wells who came promptly to her side to encourage her and help her up. Afterward, the girl clung to the black American's arm for support. However, without O'Hara, they had proceeded more steadily. A few rubber trees, very old and tall, came into sight, and the height of the causeway on which they trudged lowered markedly until it was almost at a level with the surrounding land. The rubber trees thickened. Here and there, an old rusted fence made an incongruous geometric line through the wilderness of what had been an extensive plantation of many scores of square miles. It was about three o'clock when they heard the jeeps coming.

The noise of the engines seemed alien after so many hours of chattering, cawing, squawking forest sounds. Durell halted. The others behind him sank down with groans of relief. Only Mr. Soo, among his Chinese, remained standing, listening. It would be a few moments, Durell judged, before the vehicles arrived. Sally walked up to where he stood.

"Is it over?" Her lips were swollen from insect bites. "Is it really over?"

"I think it's just begun."

"But we are all late for the auction, aren't we?"

His eyes were gentle. "You seem very tired, Sally. Don't give up yet. You'll soon be able to rest."

She sighed and shrugged. Her clothing was torn, and although her skin was the color of clear amber, she had been painfully sunburned during the hours of the afternoon.

"Atimboku is too cheerful now," she said. "Too sure of

himself. It makes me afraid of what he's planning to do. I don't understand him at all, anymore."

"Has he threatened you directly?"

"Many times. He wants to rule Pakuru alone, of course. Our old tribal ways give me a lot of power back home. Maybe he plans for me never to get back there. He laughs when I beg him to give up this whole thing."

"Don't worry, he won't get the Zero Formula."

"How can you be so confident, Sam?" When he did not reply, she smiled with sudden wistfulness. "It was so beautiful last night—in the hammock—"

He said, "Here come the Jeeps."

# 2

There was one armored scout car and two gray-painted Jeeps, each mounting a .50 mm machine gun. The Indians who manned the vehicles also carried new automatic rifles. They wore uniforms of a sort—khaki slacks, low jungle boots, white shirts, and ponchos. Their faces were hard and alert under their wide straw hats. They seemed familiar with their weapons and knew how to handle them. The scout car carried six men, and seated beside the driver was the neatly uniformed Agosto.

"Senhor Durell! Come forward, please. The rest of you stand together. Do not try anything foolish. Is it understood? Durell?"

He stepped toward the scout car. A vicious-eyed harpy eagle was tied by a length of light chain to a bar behind the windshield. The bird eyed him with ravenous hostility, and he briefly thought of Connie Drew, the girl he had contacted in Paramaguito. Agosto climbed down from the vehicle. He seemed no different from the mild-mannered agent who had joined them in Belém. His white teeth gleamed in his bronzed face.

"You are not surprised, Senhor Durell?"

"Nothing surprises me in our business. Where is O'Hara?"

"Happily drinking himself into a stupor with some bottles I provided for him. It was amusing, to see him watch you discover the old grave of your grandmother in this remote place. But of course, O'Hara was the one who buried her here, after kidnapping her and taking her with him to Brazil, where he was hired by Don Federico. These things happened many, many years ago, but his fear of vengeance always haunted him. It made him easy to handle, at times. The poor girl was ashamed to go back to your grandfather, so long ago, after O'Hara had ravished her, I suppose. Morality is different today, eh?"

"Perhaps not," Durell said.

"You still show no surprise. You have no questions? You do not wonder about me?"

"I know all about you," said Durell. "You masterminded this whole thing, didn't you? You planned our routes, tested us for your private amusement by creating problems and roadblocks for us. A game of chess, in a way. I figured, in the very beginning, there were only a few ex-intelligence officers in the business who would arrange this as you have done."

"Ah? Then you know my real name is not Agosto?"

Durell nodded. "And I know it was you who killed Andy Weyer in Belém to get on our team. The job had your particular mark of depravity on it."

"But then you know my name?"

"You've been known by many names, not just Agosto Laurentino de Mello. But you are, of course, Colonel Paolo Bom Jesus de Santana, born in Goa, India, and most recently of Portuguese Mozambique and Angola. You were the famous designer of the Lumaganga trap where some seventy-three guerilas were coldly massacred. Yes, I know you. But you didn't design the Zero Formula, did you? You arranged for the 'demonstrations' in different countries that could pay your price. You're the one who thought of the idea of an auction, to have us all bid against each other so you could market it at the highest price. You've been playing fun and games with us all. It didn't bother me, however, until you killed Andy Weyer."

Belmont had been standing nearby, listening while he watched the Indians with their rifles. The rest of the party stood in an uncertain huddle down the abandoned track. Belmont's thin face was oddly gray as Durell spoke. Then Durell saw the thin flicker of a knife slide out of Belmont's ragged sleeve, like the slither of a deadly snake. At that moment, he knew that de Santana—or Agosto—could kill Belmont as casually as slapping at a mosquito. One of the Indian guards shouted and Durell jumped to knock up Belmont's arm. The knife flashed in a pinwheel of light, almost too quick for the eye to follow. His move threw Belmont's aim off. The knife clattered harmlessly against the heavy steel of the scout car. At the same time, one of the Indians impetuously triggered his automatic rifle. The racketing noise filled the hot, stifling air. Great clouds of brilliant birds, cockatoos, parrots, bee-catchers, exploded from the surrounding trees. Monkeys screamed and fled through the vines. Everyone in the Russian party fell flat. One of Atimboku's warriors fell backward, his body stiff, and hung as if crucified in the tough vines on the rail embankment.

Colonel de Santana smiled and raised his gun and pointed it at Belmont.

"Don't," Durell said sharply.

"Why not?" Agosto was calm. "He is one of your assassins, and when a killer lets his anger control him, then he is less than worthless."

"It was my fault," Durell said.

"Why did you not let him kill me, then?"

"Because I still need you, Agosto."

"But you know I am not the man you think of as Agosto. I am sorry, but Belmont must be punished."

The gun came up again in the man's hand. It was to be an execution, senseless except to satisfy the man's vanity. Belmont stood very still, helpless, his face pale, his hands empty. At the last moment, Durell jumped. His reaching fingers managed to strike the gun in the other's hand. It went off with a shattering roar. One of the armed Indians leaped down from the scout car and clubbed Durell with his rifle, drove him to his knees. A booted foot slammed into his ribs. Pain exploded in the back of his head. Another kick slogged into his groin. He rolled over, doubling up in the weeds. Dimly he heard Inocenza scream. Or perhaps it was Sally. Mr. Soo called out a plea in a high, calm voice, and then he forced himself up to his hands and knees.

Atimboku spoke urgently behind him. "Kill him, Colonel. Do it at once, or he will destroy you, sooner or later."

"Ah, Prince Tim! You are anxious for Durell to die? He did a foolish, astonishing thing, to save his man."

"I tell you, Durell is too dangerous! You have him now, you can be rid of him——"

"Ah, but can you bid higher than he? He represents the United States Treasury, at this moment. No, no. But Belmont can be eliminated with small loss."

Durell gathered himself again and lunged at de Santana's legs. His shoulder hit the man's thigh and they both fell against the scout car. For just that moment, he saw Belmont still standing as he was. He had a good look at de Santana's face. He would not have recognized it as the formerly friendly Agosto. The man's gun was leveled at his head. The Indians had come out of their vehicles now, herding the others toward the jeeps. The pain in Durell's belly made him want to double up. He thought of Andy Weyer and the way Weyer had died. He forced himself upward and remained on his feet. Sally was crying soundlessly, the tears staining her face. Inocenza looked fascinated, black eyes wide with satisfaction.

Let it end here, he thought.

De Santana's features changed into a mask of cruel humor. Durell saw movement from one of the Indian guards. He tried to duck the blow from the rifle butt. Then he went down, his ears roaring, aware of the searing sun high above the trees. He was kicked again and again. Blood ran down his face. He struggled to get up again, and Belmont said in a strange voice, "Don't, Sam. Please. He doesn't know where the money is."

Suddenly the sun winked out and Durell fell into a deep dark place of cool silence.

# Chapter Eleven

VOICES buzzed like angry insects above and around him. He did not open his eyes. He was aware of a hammock under him, heard the hiss of a gasoline lantern that made shadows dance behind his closed lids. Someone applied a cool wet sponge to his face and squeezed a few drops on his parched lips. The sponge went down his chest and belly, wiping blood crusted on his skin. His groin, his stomach, his ribs ached. He felt as if someone had tried to tear his head off. He was naked, and he felt a momentary stir of alarm over that, too. Then someone said, "Sam? Sam, can you hear me?"

Willie Wells came in. "Leave him alone, both of you. They've brought his clothes. He's doing fine. Tony?"

"Yes," said Belmont.

"You were lucky. We'll never know what made Agosto change his mind. Go outside and make sure we're alone."

"Willie, he kept me from being shot. I owe him—"

"Go on. He'll be all right."

A door opened and closed. Moist, warm air flowed briefly over Durell's naked body. He opened his eyes, stared at a roughly timbered ceiling that showed the underside of reddish tiles through it. He looked at the hissing gasoline lamp on a wooden table and said thinly, "Turn it off."

"What, Sam?"

"Turn off the lamp."

"Right. Whatever you say. Inocenza has some water for you. And some food. They've treated us all right, so far. The auction begins tonight, in an hour. But without you, I don't know what's going to happen."

"You say they've brought back my clothes?"

"Right. Taken apart, seam by seam. Looking for your letter of credit, I figure."

"My belt?"

"It's just a belt, Sam."

"No, it isn't."

Wells turned off the gasoline lantern. Moonlight filled the dusty, broken-down room. Inocenza brought him an enameled tray with a steaming mug of coffee, a small steak, some fresh white bread, a bottle of American bourbon. She regarded his nakedness with frank approval. Durell drank part of a tumbler of bourbon first, felt its warmth curl in his belly, then settled down to the steak and bread. The flatware was antique silver, elaborately monogrammed. Willie Wells handed him his watch. In the pale light that came through the bungalow windows, he saw it was still almost an hour before midnight. The moonlight came through gaps in the plank walls as well as the broken tiles of the roof. Everything was ebony and silver.

"They've started the bidding," Willie Wells said. "It's going on in the main plantation house."

"How is Belmont?"

"Sitting outside. Agosto didn't kill him, after you were knocked out. Are you sure you're okay, Cajun?"

"I'm fine. I heard you, Willie. The bidding has started. There is no hurry. How many got here?"

"Almost twenty. Make it eighteen. You've got a funny look on your face, Cajun."

Durell poured himself another drink and finished the hot coffee with it. The bungalow they were in was roughly framed and timbered, showing some new repairs. It had obviously once been used as one of several bunkhouses on the old rubber plantation. Some effort had been made to refurbish and clean it up. There were straw rugs on the broomed floor, fresh linen on the bunks, a new plastic-topped table with folding legs and rattan chairs. Durell swung his legs carefully out of the lower bunk he was in and stood up. The room swung in a slow, dizzying circle around him for a moment. Inocenza looked concerned, but did not touch him. Then his vision steadied. He reached for his slacks, checked the wide black leather belt he had constantly worn. The seams had been partly ripped open as he expected, but the buckle and button attachment seemed to be intact.

"Give me a rundown, Willie."

The black man sat down on one of the wall bunks. "They had a doctor, of sorts, to look you over. No real damage, he said. You know you broke all the rules, busting loose like that for Belmont."

Durell walked to one of the square windows. The moonlight showed him a large compound with other bungalows scattered about. There was a horse corral, the dark loom of old rubber trees ranged in linear patterns as far into the gloom as he could see. A black strip of metal was just in the leftward limit of his vision. He swore softly. "Is that an airstrip, Willie?"

"Yup. There's a hangar holding a helicopter—a Bell, I think—and a Cessna six-seater. Some of the other bidders were flown in. De Santana's sense of humor sure got us here the hard way."

"Any sign of a radio transmitter?"

"Couldn't see much when we got here. They hustled us into this bungalow, locked the door for a while, sent in the Indian medic to look at you, then left us alone. The whole place is run like a military camp, seems like. That would be de Santana's habit, from fighting terrorists in Portuguese East Africa, I reckon. But I saw some aerial wires on the main house—a big old hacienda, red tile roof, looking recently spruced up a bit, although one wing came tumbling down long ago. They've got a diesel generator in a separate building about fifty yards in this direction. So the radio, if there is one, must work, and there's power for a big house, so they can contact their planes. There's a newly built shed attached to the main house, too, that might be a laboratory. The thing is, Cajun, nobody has even offered a guess as to who actually invented the Zero Formula. It's a sure bet it wasn't Colonel Paolo Bom Jesus de Santana. Nothing in his dossier ever showed any studies in biological engineering."

Durell nodded. The whiskey and the food had helped to settle his stomach and end the slight vertigo he had felt.

His ribs seemed intact, but there was a massive ache in his belly where he had been kicked. He went to the door, limping a bit, and opened it to look out at the night. A shadow stood up from the weeds beside the entrance.

"Belmont?"

"Yo, Sam. I want to thank you."

"No need. Where is the main house?"

"That way. Are you okay?"

Durell rubbed the back of his neck. "I've felt better. How many of these Indians do you guess there are?"

"Forty, maybe fifty. They're all armed with Russian rifles, Kalashnikovs, and some Israeli Uzis. They're spooked to the eyes. Don't make any sudden moves near them, Cajun."

"Any chance of grabbing some weapons?"

"Not right now. I tell you, they're alert."

Durell looked to the left. The old plantation's original sheds, warehouses and outbuildings had long yielded to the implacable hunger of the Amazon wilderness, but the main house, on a small knoll, was brightly lighted in the central area. The shadows of armed Indian guards moved steadily in a tight perimeter around the building. There were other bunkhouses similar to the one to which they had been assigned, all around the compound. He wondered which one contained Sally. Beyond the clearing, the forest of rubber trees made a dark wall of forgotten cultivation in the moonlight. The airstrip was only a quarter of a mile away. The hangar doors were shut. The guards were alert there, too.

Belmont said softly, "Did Willie tell you the bidding has started, Sam? Looks like we've been left out of it."

"Not likely. Who else is here, exactly?"

"Damnedest collection I've ever seen. The British are here, represented by Major Philip Stokes-Hawley. Number Two man in their G-6. And Pierre Armand Polineaux, Sûreté. There's a Yugoslav, an East German, and Herr Schumann from Bonn's BfV, the Bundesant fur Verfassunsschutz. Prince Atimboku Mari Mak Mujilikaka, of course. Very cocky. A Swede I don't know, all pious idealism to save the world's ecology. Mr. Soo, playing the inscrutable Oriental. The Russians, with Vodaniev now all smiles and heavy-handed peasant anecdotes like Khrushchev used to be." Belmont shook his head. His eyes were sunk deep in his face. "A dozen others. All top intelligence people. There's never been anything like it, Sam."

"And Guerlan Stepanic?"

"Him, too. But the others ignore him." Belmont paused. "Sam, they picked your clothes apart like they were looking for nits, then sewed 'em up again. Did they get your letter of credit?"

"No."

"Then where is it?"

"In my belt. It's double-stitched."

Belmont's face was shadowed in the moonlight. "But they've started without you, Sam."

"No problem," Durell said.

He waited. He was accustomed to waiting, in this business. He sat outside the bungalow door and watched the moonlight on the compound. The place was full of ghosts. Indian slave labor, tapping the trees under the eyes of watchful, brutal guards; the clank of machinery and the slosh of the precious sap in great vats under the corrugated tin roofs of the warehouses; the fine, elegant parties that Don Federico held in his sumptuous plantation house. It had been a world of incredible wealth and luxury built upon the bones of desolate misery. Durell watched the Indians pace stolidly around the bungalows. They eyed him curiously, but did not come close when he called softly to them. Their eyes gleamed like liquid silver in the hot, tropical night. He waited another ten minutes. Some of the bruising aches in him began to ease off. The other bungalows were dark and silent. Again he wondered which one was occupied by Atimboku and Sally. Then a jeep motor started up behind the big house. Headlights flared, dimming his night vision. He began walking toward the plantation house. To his left was the airstrip, well guarded. He got no more than ten paces from the bungalow when two guards stopped him. Their flat faces were hard and sullen.

"No, senhor," one of them said. "You must stay."

"I want to see the boss."

"He has been advised that you are awake and well. He comes now."

In a few moments, the jeep halted beside him.

## 2

The bald man had an air of decay, as if some of the leprous rot of the old plantation had invaded his being. The first swift impression Durell had was that of a terrified but desperate man. He looked as if he once had been stout and jolly, but the Amazon had wasted him, eroding flesh and muscle, so that his white silk suit, which should have been elegant, now hung on his medium frame in shapeless lumps and folds. He wore round, silver-rimmed glasses, and one of the side frames had been broken and impatiently repaired with a strip of black electrician's tape, as if he couldn't be bothered by getting new frames. Behind the glasses, his eyes were bright and owlish, but oddly incurious. He was middle-aged, with a sallow, fevered skin and a two-day stubble of gray beard. There was a thin shine of sweat on his bald skull and upper lip.

"We are having a brief intermission, Mr. Durell. So far, the bidding has been a disappointment."

"What did you expect?"

"I truly regret that Colonel Agosto gave you the most difficult route to follow. He enjoys his little games."

"And he has his own brand of humor."

"I also regret the violence that caused your injuries. It was your fault, the colonel says. A gallant but foolish gesture to keep an assistant of yours from harm. Do you feel better now?"

"A bit."

"You are prepared to join the others?"

"I'm curious. How high has the bidding gone?"

"Only eight million in the equivalent of your American dollars. We will certainly accept not less than one hundred million, and we expect much, much more. The colonel and I will not allow you to conspire with the others to hold down the bidding. If necessary, we are ready with other demonstrations of the Zero Formula, to convince your various governments that we are indeed in earnest. I told the colonel that all the rigmarole of your arrival here was unnecessary. But as I said, he enjoys his somewhat devious amusements."

"Yes," Durell said. "You are from Prague?"

"Ah. You have an ear for accents."

"The Russians took you away over ten years ago. How did you get to this place?"

"I escaped. I was more physically active, then."

"Then you are Professor Anton Tovachek. You've won several prizes for biological engineering."

"Ah. That was a long time ago." There was a sad, small smile on the man's face. "Will you have more coffee? More food? We are all lost here in this wild land, but we do manage some amenities."

"Thank you, no."

"You need not fear poison or hypnotics, or anything like that."

Durell shook his head. There was a box of thin Brazilian cigars on the steel desk. He didn't ordinarily smoke, but he took one and lit it in order to have a moment in which to listen and look around him. The room smelled as decayed as his small, weary host. It had been rebuilt within the ruined shell of the plantation house, but in the brief glimpse he'd had when escorted in here, he realized that much of the hacienda was still only a hollow frame, filled with dust and broken furniture that had withstood the termites and a half-century of Amazon rain and heat. The natural vermin had been cleaned out, only to be replaced by this small man whose once-brilliant mind now threatened to crush the fragile ecology of the world. Some men existed and thrived only amid violence and disorder. Colonel Paolo de Santana was such a man, a parasite feeding on death. Durell was not sure about this quiet-spoken little Czech, however. There could be only one explanation about their strange, symbiotic relationship. Professor Tovachek was not a predator like Agosto. They were worlds apart.

He smoked his cigar carefully.

"How long have you been working here, professor?"

"Eight years, Mr. Durell."

"With Agosto, all this time?"

"No, no. Agosto, as you call him, appeared only two years ago. I had been hiding, you understand, since my escape from the Soviet Union. I killed a man, you see. No, that is not true. I killed three men. And killed myself, and my hopes, in doing so, one might say. Are you sure you will not have more coffee? We have ten minutes left."

"Are the police after you?"

The small man nodded. His glasses glinted in the light of his desk lamp. Durell settled back in a large rattan chair. The professor said, "I was utterly desperate. One of the men I had to kill to escape the KGB, who wanted me back, was a Brazilian police officer who recognized me. I could not afford to be discovered. I wished to be thought of as dead and beyond the reach of the men who rule this world. So I became a fugitive. Behind the Iron Curtain, they hold alive my wife and two children as hostages against my return." The man's hands made despairing arabesques in the hot, midnight air. A great moth began to flutter in circles around the desk lamp. Its iridescent wings flickered and flashed around the Czech's bald head. He paid it no attention. "Mine is a familiar tale, I fear. I wished only to continue my work, to find some way to stem the growth of human population that threatens to cause desperate eruptions on this earth, sooner than most of us realize. Some unexpected benefits began to turn up out of my experiments in controlling undesirable crop and foliage growths. I found this place where no man comes, you see, and finished my work on the Zero Formula."

"Who discovered you here and took care of you?"

"It was O'Hara."

"O'Hara brought you here?"

"For a certain sum of money. I managed to bank a maintenance sum in Manaus, and another in Belém. As long as I could pay O'Hara, I was safe here. The Indians, especially, were very kind to me."

"But your money ran out," Durell suggested.

"Yes."

"So then O'Hara brought Agosto here."

"Yes."

"And you have been Agosto's prisoner ever since?"

"In a sense. Yes."

"And your whole scheme to auction off the formula is really Agosto's idea?"

"I am not innocent. I will not pretend to be. I want the money. A vast fortune can be turned into a fortress. Agosto promises he can buy my wife and children out to safety." The small man was agitated now. He took off his glasses and wiped them. The big circling moth made wildly flickering shadows on the walls of the room. Its great wings were purple and gold flecked with bright oculi of red. It was coming dangerously close to the lamp. Professor Tovachek's hands, stained indelibly by chemicals, shook as he replaced his silver-rimmed glasses. Durell was aware of the big armed Indian who stood impassively in the doorway at his back. A bell rang somewhere within the ruined house, and he heard distant footsteps, a low murmur of masculine voices. The professor stood up jerkily. "We must go. Agosto is angry with the bidding, so far."

Durell said, "Professor, we can make a deal."

"No, no."

"Just between us."

"The guard understands English, Senhor Durell."

"He can be bought."

"Please, I—no, no, it is impossible."

"You can have your millions. As many as you need. Royalties, subsidiary rights in patents to your device. All legitimate. If you accept our protection, you will find that the United States is a large, free country."

"Wherever I tried to hide, I would be found. The colonel would find me. He would kill my wife and children first. He could arrange it. He can arrange anything. You do not know him. Then he would find me and kill me, too."

The bell rang again. The Indian came forward from the doorway and prodded Durell with his rifle. He stood up and followed Professor Anton from the room. He knew very well that his offer had been monitored and taped somewhere. Perhaps even televised by the tiny camera he had spotted behind one of the dusty Victorian hangings that covered the window.

Agosto was probably thinking about it right now.

He looked back for a moment into the room. The big, beautiful moth had finally grazed the hot electric bulb and singed one of his wings. It lay fluttering in helpless, tormented circles on top of the desk. It would soon be dead.

### 3

In the rich years of the rubber boom, the Amazon land barons who ruled the wilderness lived in extravagant luxury in this place so remote from civilization. Remnants of the feudal mode of life practiced by the plantation owners had resisted the ravages of time and weather, insect and mold. The room to which Durell was ushered had once been a private theater, an opera house in miniature, where plays and performers had been imported from Europe and the States simply for the personal entertainment of Don Federico and his select neighbors. The hall occupied the central section of the upper level of the sprawling hacienda. There was a stage lighted by garish, naked bulbs that occasionally flickered with the rhythm of the diesel generator; there were boxes and a small row of gilded chairs from which the velvet had long since disintegrated. Draperies hung in dusty, tattered rags, ready to fall apart at a touch. The original paint had been ivory and gold, with cupids whose wings and faces had been eaten away by termites, curlicues of gilt, oil lanterns and a brilliant crystal chandelier which had long ago fallen from the domed ceiling, which still lay in twinkling splinters in the central aisle. Up front, there were about twenty men, formally seated, their backs to Durell.

The stage was empty for the moment.

It was odd, Durell thought, to be in the same room with men who would have been greatly pleased to kill him. Dr. Soo, of Peking, turned a bland, faintly inquiring face toward him as he took a seat up forward. Vladim Vodaniev looked at him with open malevolence, obviously disappointed that Durell had turned up at all. Atimboku grinned, displaying superb confidence. The British and the French, from the DST, sat together and talked in earnest undertones. The West German representative from the BFV stolidly smoked a pipe. There were a Pakistani, a Bulgarian obviously chosen to help the Russians manipulate the bidding, and others whose names and faces flickered in Durell's memory like a spinning card file. Each of these men were among the best in the business, commanding intelligence teams of agents the world over, in the silent, deadly war that avowed no rules, that allowed no mistakes. Their profession had made them a breed apart—dangerous, quick, solitary, trained to conceal and evade, to pursue their way relentlessly toward their various goals. Information was the costliest commodity in the world today, and these men were all experts at obtaining it by subversion, suborning innocent lives, degrading and blackmailing their victims, using people as puppets, as units in some terrible computerized game where the individual's humanity meant nothing, and the data counted for all.

Tension coiled in the room, entrapping all those within as if in the deadly embrace of a giant anaconda. At each door leading into the ghostly theater, the Indian guards stood stolidly with their arms ready. The men in the chairs before the stage were prisoners, willing or not. Nothing could ever be the same in this remote spot, where Professor Anton hoped for so much.

There was a brief wait. No one spoke.

Presently two Indians with sidearms rolled a chart of the world onto the platform. It was similar to the one that Homer Carboyd had displayed back in Maryland, after Durell had seen the damage done at George's Fields. Then Colonel Paolo de Santana entered the stage, smiling his gentle assassin's smile. He placed a heavy target pistol on a small lectern before him and kept his hand on it.

"Gentlemen," he said softly.

No one replied.

"Gentlemen, we all know each other. And every one of you knows that we are most disappointed in the first bidding for Professor Tovachek's Zero Formula. You know that the formula may be used for good or evil. Your governments, without exception, do not make international morality their prime consideration, however. I know that each of you has orders to bid a maximum amount to obtain the formula and return with it to your respective governments. We will tolerate no conspiracies among you to keep the price down. You are under heavy guard. Until this business here is resolved, none of you may leave the plantation alive."

Mr. Soo coughed gently. "On behalf of the People's Republic of China, I protest your statement regarding the morality of socialist use of your device. I cannot speak for the representatives of Western imperialist, expansionist powers or East European revisionist nations, but—"

"Mr. Soo."

De Santana's voice was soft, like a sheath of velvet covering cold steel.

"Mr. Soo, dialectical polemics and propaganda have no value here. We are all businessmen in a sense, professionals of the highest order in our craft. That is why each of you was requested specifically to attend this auction. The hour is late. Let us go on with it. Who will pay ten million for the formula? Prince Atimboku?"

"Yes. Ten million."

"Fifteen," said the Bulgarian.

"Sixteen," said Mr. Soo.

"Nonsense," Vodaniev rumbled. "Twenty million."

Colonel de Santana smiled coldly. "Gentlemen, we are still speaking of pin money. If none of you is serious, we will close the bidding for tonight. A good night's sleep, and reflection on your duty to your various employers, may grant you enlightenment in the morning."

Vodaniev stood up. "One moment, please."

"Yes?"

"We have discussed so far only how much you expect for the formula that Professor Tovachek—a defector and a traitor, a scum of a man, I might add—has devised. Impossible sums. True, the effectiveness of the Zero Formula has been demonstrated to us. That is why our governments have sent us here. No one wishes to be among the last generation of life on earth. Such a device must be adequately controlled by sane and reasonable men, acting in the interests of a socialist society. It must not become the property of any expansionist, capitalist nation to use and exploit others. It must not—"

"Tut, tut, Comrade Vodaniev."

"*Da*. Well. You have not spoken of guarantees."

"Gentlemen, the man who bids and wins the Zero Formula, the party whose letter of credit is satisfactorily honored and redeemed—a matter of only a day or two to verify, I assure you—will receive complete protection while here. Once the money has been safely transferred and is in the control of my agents abroad, the owner of the Zero Formula will, under adequate guard, be escorted by plane from this place to any destination he chooses. All the others must remain here under close watch for a period of forty-eight hours before being permitted to leave. No attempt to steal the formula from the winning bidder will be permitted. Is that satisfactory?"

Vladim Vodaniev remained stubbornly on his feet. His round, pudgy face was adamant.

"Not quite, Colonel. We know your record. We know your tricks. You are like the bad penny that always turns up in the till. Your record stinks of deceit and treachery. How can we know that the winner of the Zero Formula will have the one and exclusive copy of it?"

"There is only one copy now," de Santana said softly. "This entire place and the laboratory will be burned to the ground before anyone leaves. Inspection and search of our persons and the premises will be permitted." De Santana smiled paternally. "There will be no written, taped, or recorded copy of the data in existence except that which the winner will receive."

Atimboku called impatiently from his seat. "I wish to bid thirty million."

"Thank you, sir."

"Thirty-five," said the Bulgarian.

Mr. Soo said, "Thirty-six."

De Santana turned to where Durell sat. "You are not bidding, sir?"

"No," Durell said.

"The USA does not wish to possess the one and only copy of the formula? Perhaps to—ah—use to keep the world safe for democracy?"

There was a stir and a snicker from some of the others. Durell was impassive. "I am not bidding."

"Not at all?"

"Not yet."

"Ah."

De Santana looked puzzled for a moment, then urged the others to continue. Durell waited and watched. His head throbbed, his ribs and belly ached. He did not wish to be the one to ask the inevitable question that must occur. The bidding reached fifty-five million. Atimboku's black, hawk's face was covered with a thin sheen of sweat. Standing on the stage behind the lectern, de Santana seemed to be in excellent humor now. Durell wished for a drink and an aspirin. He felt the toll of the long trek from São Felice more than the others, considering the beating he had taken to save Belmont. The air grew hot and stale in the decayed splendor of the little theater. It was past one o'clock in the morning. Now and then the others gave him curious, puzzled glances. He wished for a cold shower, a few hours of sleep in a clean bed with crisp sheets.

He waited.

Mr. Soo stood up.

"One more question, Colonel de Santana."

"Certainly, Mr. Soo."

"There will always be, within his lifetime, one who could recreate the formula and perhaps sell it to someone else. Another copy, so to speak, in the mind of another man."

"Yes. I have anticipated such a query. I wish to prove

to you my earnest desire to satisfy you. You refer, of course, to Professor Anton Tovachek, whose brilliant brain conceived the Zero Formula and who could, of course, recreate it again, at any time."

"Precisely," said Mr. Soo.

From offstage, as if on cue, came a dim shout.

De Santana said, "The winner of the formula takes Professor Anton with him, of course."

Now the shout offstage became a muffled cry of denial. There was something inevitable about what followed, Durell thought. It was as if all the events that had brought them to this ghostly place were foreordained, like the elemental movements of a Greek tragedy. Professor Anton came onto the stage. His arms flapped in his dirty white silk suit. His silver-rimmed glasses glinted on his pinched nose. His face was gray. He did not look at any of the men seated in the small theater. He walked to the lectern, staggering slightly, and confronted de Santana.

"What are you saying?" he shouted. "How dare you make such a proposal? Everything I have done has been meant to keep my freedom. I did not offer myself as a prisoner! What good would the money do to me, if I rot in a cell somewhere in China or Russia or Africa? Nothing of this was ever discussed between us—"

"But my dear professor, logic makes such an agreement utterly necessary."

"I do *not* agree!" Anton shouted. He turned and looked out from the stage, his eyes blinking behind his round glasses. His face worked curiously. There was a trapped expression in his frantic eyes. He was a man betrayed, appealing for justice. But no one among the bidders reacted to his pathetic gestures, his silent and futile arm-flapping, his appeals for help and understanding. The full extent of his betrayal slowly convulsed his features. He looked as if he were going to weep. He stood under the light on the stage and began to shiver.

"It is true." His whisper was like the ghost of the wind that moved among the ancient rubber trees on the plantation. "Yes, true. I created the formula, and I can create it again. When I worked on it and tested it, it was not my purpose to terrorize the world with its results. Quite the opposite. I meant to give it to all mankind for peaceful purposes, in exchange for my freedom from pursuit and the freedom of my family. None of the trickery that was devised to bring you people here was of my invention." He flapped his arms again, and now sweat poured down his round face. "What would I know of your world, gentlemen? How would I know your names and positions? It was the colonel who arranged it all, who shipped samples to your countries, who hired men to spray from planes and trucks." Anton paused and gulped. His eyes were like a toad's behind his round glasses. His sudden courage gave way to a quivering of his chin. He straightened in his pathetically oversized clothes and stared at them all. "There is only one copy of the formula. That is true. But whoever thinks he will have a monopoly on the Zero Formula is mistaken. Not by taking me with it."

He tapped his head. "It is all here. In my brain. I have had enough of this monstrous charade. The colonel has a streak of madness in him, sirs. I suggest we end this so-called auction. I shall give each of you a copy of the formula, and in this way, the world will remain in balance for a while longer. I suggest that you ignore the colonel's offer to purchase what I can give you freely."

Professor Anton Tovachek stopped talking. There was a long silence in the dusty theater. It went on for too long. No one looked at each other. *It won't work,* Durell thought grimly. The little man was fighting for his life, but these men were dedicated to their work, to the needs of their respective countries. They had come here in rivalry for one purpose only. The piteous plea fell on deaf ears. These men were not altruistic. They were here under compulsion, each an alien island to the others, each a wary predator cast against his will among other predators. But Durell did not expect the reaction that followed.

Colonel de Santana smiled his gentle smile, picked up his heavy target pistol from the lectern, and crossed the stage to where Anton stood.

Then he placed the muzzle of the gun to the back of Anton's head and pulled the trigger.

The report was calamitous in the little theater. Dust jumped. Some plaster fell. The bullet blasted through the back of the professor's skull and blew out bone, brains, one eye, tissue and blood from the man's face. Some of the human debris spattered the bidders in the front row of seats. Anton was dead before he hit the floor. Atimboku jumped aside with a small yelp. No one else moved or said anything. No one voiced an objection. De Santana calmly replaced his gun on the lecturn and kept his hand on it.

"Gentlemen, you have just been delivered your guarantee. I have the only copy of the Zero Formula. It cannot be reproduced any more by *that*." He gestured to the body below the old stage. "Whoever wins the formula may also burn this place down." He turned slightly. "Mucujai?"

One of the guards stirred at the left end of the stage. He was a big man, broad-shouldered, with a dark coppery face. Durell saw that of all the people in this place, only the Indians seemed shocked by what had happened.

"Mucujai, take the body away."

"*Sim,* Senhor Colonel."

The Indian's voice was gravelly with open resentment. He had short-cropped gray hair and a long jaw. His shock did not keep him from obeying the order, however; and he chose another assistant from among the armed guards to help him. Agosto was silent, watching them depart with their burden. Then he smiled with great good humor again.

"Are there any other questions, gentlemen?"

"Yes."

"Mr. Soo?"

The Chinese said, "We have seen and learned much about you, Colonel. How can we trust *you*? You said you have no other copy, here or elsewhere, but how can we know that?"

"Ah?"

"You could offer that copy of the formula for sale, later, as a form of further blackmail, I should think."

Agosto suddenly looked impatient. "Surely you must realize that I haven't told you the entire truth. Of course I have another copy, Mr. Soo. Am I stupid enough to trust you? The extra copy is to guarantee my personal safety. If anything happens to me after this meeting, the Zero Formula *will* become public knowledge, and the bidder will have spent his nation's money uselessly. One can only guess at the penalties that might befall such a man then. The extra copy is not here. There is no point in wondering where it might be. Perhaps on the other side of the world. But if any harm comes to me, then the penalty will be paid. The formula will be published."

Durell spoke up. "You're bluffing, Agosto."

"Ah! The American speaks. The poker player, eh?"

Durell said, "If you have another copy elsewhere, one that will be published automatically if you are killed, then all of us who lose in the bidding will see that you die promptly, to keep the winner from gaining a monopoly on the Zero Formula. So either way, Agosto, you will lose."

This time there was a murmur of sardonic amusement from the gathering. Agosto sensed that he had momentarily lost control. His face darkened with anger, and he raised his heavy pistol for a moment, then lowered it.

"There is an answer for you, Mr. Durell. You are very clever. And more dangerous than I thought. But, I assure you, there is an answer. We will adjourn until tomorrow morning, gentlemen. The hour is late. We will resume our business at 0800 sharp. The guards will escort you back to your quarters."

# Chapter Twelve

IT WAS well past one o'clock in the morning. Durell felt weariness and pain drag at him as he spoke to Inocenza in the bungalow. The gasoline lantern was turned off, but the moonlight outlined the girl's rich and sullen mouth. She looked defiant. Belmont slept on the floor, rejecting the bunks. Willie Wells, lounging against the door, watched a small red lizard dart along a broken rafter in the dim ceiling.

"Don't bully her, Sam," Wells said softly.

"I want to know where O'Hara is."

"How can she know that?"

"She knows. O'Hara has been here before."

"What do you want with the old man? His crime against your grandmother was long ago, Cajun."

Durell shook his head. "We need O'Hara. You see, I gave Agosto no choice. I brought it all out into the open."

"What do you mean?"

"I argued him into a box. He has no alternative now. Whoever wins the formula goes free."

"But you didn't bid, you say."

"I had my reasons. According to Agosto's plan, the rest of us will be killed. It's the only way he can come out of this alive, without one of us killing him to release his copy of the formula to the whole world. He made a mistake by admitting his 'insurance.' He can only be safe now by eliminating all the losers and burying us here in the forest."

Inocenza whispered, "He will kill *all* of us?"

"He must. It's his only way out."

"Do the Russians and Mr. Soo know this?" Willie asked.

"I'm sure they've figured it out already. We're all dead

men, except for the one who pays Agosto's price—and then becomes Agosto's blackmail victim in the future."

Inocenza's dark face turned from Wells to Durell. "And what do you want O'Hara for?"

"I need his help, or we'll all be executed tomorrow. I won't hurt him."

"Do you promise?"

"I promise."

"Very well," she said. "How do we go past the guards? They are very nervous now, since the professor was shot."

"You can help me with that, too."

It worked well enough. Inocenza opened the door and stepped out of the bungalow. The night was darker now; the moon was ready to set. The moment she appeared, one of the Indian guards jumped up and jabbed her backward with his rifle. The girl spoke angrily in a mixture of Portuguese and Tupamaca dialect. The Indian grinned and began to laugh and made an obscene gesture with his fingers on his buttocks. Inocenza spat at him and started across the compound toward a clump of tall bamboo. Her hips swayed provocatively. The Indian turned to watch her. The moment he did so, Durell came through the bungalow doorway and hit him in the back of the neck, stabbed two fingers into the base of the man's spine. The Indian made a low grunting sound as his knees buckled and he pitched forward. Durell caught the Russian-made rifle before it clattered to the ground. He chopped once at the side of the guard's throat, and was satisfied that the man was out.

"Willie?" he whispered. "Take care of him. Keep him quiet and keep him out of sight."

Wells said, "We've got one rifle now, anyway."

"We'll get more," Durell promised.

Inocenza vanished into the thicket of bamboo. He waited a moment to make sure there was no alarm, then ran across the dark compound after her. The effort made his right leg ache from a bruise he hadn't known was there.

The girl's whisper was hardly more than the rustle of the spiky bamboo leaves overhead.

"This way, Sam."

Her dark face was only a blur in the gloom, but through the tall bamboo stems he could see a pale sprinkle of tropical stars.

"What did you tell the guard?" he asked softly.

She giggled and he touched her lips to be sure she was careful about noise. "I said a lady needed some privacy now and then for personal matters." She added, "O'Hara has a woman here—one of the Indian girls of these guards. He told me they have some shacks down in the rubber trees. Most of these Tupamara people are descendents of the old *seringueros*—the rubber-tappers who were once slaves for Don Federico."

She moved as silently and sinuously as a forest creature, leading the way through to the other side of the bamboo thicket. Most of the lights were out in the main house now, but floodlamps strategically illuminated a perimeter where shadowy guards patrolled. A small wind moved in the tops of the old trees. There was a path of sorts, winding between the gnarled, twisted trunks. She held his hand and drew him along after her. The forest was silent. Presently there was a clearing among the thickly bunched trees and he made out the shapes of a few raggedly built huts, scattered at random here and there.

From one of the nearest huts came the sound of O'Hara's grating voice, mumbling or singing something. A woman spoke softly and patiently to him. Durell remembered the fat old Indian woman at Paramaguito, and wondered at the old man's toughness. A faint light inside showed him a patchily screened window and the outline of a door.

"He never seems to sleep," Inocenza whispered.

"Stay here," he suggested.

"No. If he yells, you will have the other Indians down on you. They will surely kill you. But if he sees me, he may be quiet. If he is not too drunk, or too frightened of you."

They moved soundlessly through the darkness to the door of the hut. A bottle clinked. There was a gurgling noise. O'Hara's voice rumbled, complaining in the Tupamara dialect, and the woman crooned soothingly. Durell put up a hand to keep Inocenza motionless and reached for the door handle and then yanked it wide open and leaped into the single-room cabin. He glimpsed two hammocks, an old oil stove, a lantern smothered with suicidal insects. The woman lay naked in one of the hammocks. She looked very young. O'Hara's back was toward him as the old man stooped to choose another bottle from among several in a wooden box. Durell got his left arm around O'Hara's throat and his right hand clamped over the man's bearded mouth before O'Hara was even aware that he had come in. Inocenza took care of the young Indian woman, holding her in the hammock. O'Hara's thick body heaved convulsively and Durell tightened his arm across the fat man's larynx and whispered, "Hold still or you're dead, *Capitão.*"

For a moment, O'Hara continued to struggle. He tightened his arm again. O'Hara made a choking sound and let himself sag down on all fours, panting.

Durell said, "I don't want to hurt you, *Capitão.* Listen to me. We're all dead men here if we don't help each other. Agosto will kill all of us. Nobody will be allowed to leave here alive, except those he chooses. You and I won't be the lucky ones. Understand?"

O'Hara moved his round, bearded head slightly. His fat stomach heaved.

"Do you understand?" Durell repeated.

"I—can't—"

"We'll just talk. I need some help."

"Okay."

Durell released his grip and stepped back warily. For some moments, O'Hara remained on all fours, coughing and choking and shaking his head. The Indian girl in the hammock peered at them with enormous dark eyes. Inocenza looked watchful. O'Hara turned his head toward her. "You brought him here, baby?"

"For your own good. Agosto is a crazy man."

"It's true, he'll kill everybody so there won't be any witnesses?"

"Durell tells the truth."

"Shit. Durell wants to get me because of his old grandma. He found her grave. He don't believe I loved her. It drove me crazy, all these years. I took her with me to the Amazon, but she wouldn't ever have any part of me. I begged and cried and told her how much I wanted her. But she got sick with the fever right away and died on me."

Durell said, "I believe you, O'Hara."

The fat old man scrunched around and sat upright on his buttocks, glaring at Durell from under his shaggy brows. A drool of spittle ran from his open, panting mouth. Fear and doubt clouded his rheumy eyes.

"I always knew one of you would come here for me."

"It's not like that," Durell said.

"What do you want from me?"

"Do you know that Professor Anton Tovachek was shot?"

"Yeah," O'Hara said. "The Indians are talking about it. They say Agosto killed him, plain cold."

"It's true. How do the Indians feel about it?"

O'Hara jerked a thumb toward the naked girl in the hammock. "Ask her. They're kinda upset about it."

"Did they like the professor?"

"They took care of him like a mascot for a few years before Agosto showed up. Sure, they liked him."

"Are they angry at the way Agosto killed him?"

O'Hara grunted and squinted up at Durell's tall figure and then slowly climbed to his feet, hitching his dirty white trousers up over his big belly. He pointed to the naked girl again.

"Her brother's name is Mucujai. He's kind of a chief among these *seringueros*. They're homeless, the last of their tribe. They never wanted trouble here. They've been upset ever since Agosto first showed up, but they did what he told them, building the airstrip and fixing up the bunkhouses and the old hacienda, only because the professor and Agosto seemed friendly enough."

"Mucujai is one of Agosto's guards, right?"

"Yeah. One of the Indian leaders."

"He's angry now?"

"I reckon so."

"Angry enough to turn against Agosto?"

O'Hara squinted at Durell again, looked at the Indian girl, and a slow grin spread in his ragged gray beard. He wiped his mouth with the back of his hand. "What you're proposing needs a drink to think on it."

"Later. Inocenza?"

The girl looked frightened. "I'm not so sure——"

"Talk to this Indian woman about it. And put some clothes on her."

O'Hara said, "She don't bother me none."

"Inocenza, ask her about the Indians and her brother. Can we talk safely to Mucujai? Or will he put us under guard again?"

"You take a big risk, Sam," she whispered.

"It's better than just sitting around waiting for a firing squad."

## 2

O'Hara stumbled and cursed and fell into a bog up to his knees. Mucujai pulled him out easily, his powerful muscles bunched with smooth tension. The moon had set, and only the tropical stars, spinning overhead, guided them. But the Indian moved familiarly along the narrow forest trail, a dry snaking path that reminded Durell of the chenieres in the Louisiana bayous, when he was a boy. Mucujai spoke in accented Portuguese.

"Are you feeling well, Senhor *Capitão?*"

"Yeah, yeah. I'm just a little drunk, I guess."

"Let me help you, Senhor *Capitão.*"

"I don't need any help," O'Hara snarled.

They walked through the tangle of old rubber trees for fifteen minutes. Mucujai had not said yes or no to Durell's proposal. He had been asleep when O'Hara led Durell to one of the shacks, but he had come awake like a cat, reaching for his gun, then freezing as he looked into the muzzle of Durell's stolen rifle. O'Hara had spoken quickly in his rusty, grating voice. Mucujai had nodded, but his flat coppery face yielded nothing. Durell could not guess what the man was thinking. But apparently there was to be no immediate resistance.

A small tributary stream into the river had overflowed during the recent rain, and water shimmered everywhere around the thick trunks of the rubber trees. Their progress was marked by small splashings and stumblings and O'Hara's virulent curses. Inocenza clung to Durell's arm, but there was no hint of the original sexuality in the gestures she made. When they came to a sudden clearing in the forest, Mucujai extended an arm and halted.

"What is this place?" Durell asked.

"Old slave quarters," O'Hara rumbled. He belched loudly. "Mucujai is the grandson of one of the old chiefs whose tribe was practically wiped out, dying as forced laborers for Don Federico. These are the old *seringuero* barracks—what's left of 'em. Mucujai and his people think this place is sacred, for some reason. Best stay here, boy. Let him go on alone."

The big Indian did not look back at them as he strode into the clearing. There were only mounds, covered with vines and grass, where the old structures had been. A larger mound, a few collapsed storage buildings, had melted into the jungle growth until they were almost undistinguishable. But the old railroad had terminated near here, judging from the higher elevation of an unmistakeable causeway that still arrowed straight through the surrounding swamp.

Durell waited patiently while the Indian stood still in the center of the circle of old mounds. It was still three hours to dawn. He hoped Belmont and Wells could keep any inquisitive guards from noting his absence from the bungalow.

Ten minutes passed. Mucujai did not change his rigid standing posture. The forest around them was silent.

Then Mucujai returned silently to where they stood.

"Senhor Durell, it was a bad thing that the colonel did, to kill our friend the professor."

"It was very bad. It was a senseless thing."

"Yes. But it is not for me to understand. The professor was a kind man. He was good to us. We were starving here in the forest, living like animals, before he came. He gave us work and money, and he had *Capitão* O'Hara bring in new blankets and hammocks and tools for us to build with. This was a good thing, and we thanked Jesus for sending the professor to help us. In return, we did what we could for him. He was not a man who could live easily in the forest. We did not know that the colonel would kill him so cruelly."

"The colonel is an evil man," Durell said.

"I believe this."

"You will be abandoned, to die in slow misery, if he has his way with us before he leaves."

Mucujai said, "We can take care of ourselves now. But the colonel must pay for killing the professor."

"How many of your people feel as you do?"

For the first time, the Indian showed indecision. "Some. Not all. One brother might fight against another."

"I do not wish that," Durell said carefully. "But we will need guns, and some of your men."

"I can get this," Mucujai said.

"If we do it quickly, and cleverly, not many will be hurt or killed."

"The professor must be avenged," Mucujai said solemnly. "I will speak to certain of the men. And get the guns. But it is a bad thing."

"It will be worse for us all, if we do not act."

"I understand this, too, senhor."

### 3

Willie Wells said, "It's going to be bloody, man."

Belmont said, "Just promise me that I can have Agosto; that's all I want."

"I can't promise anything," Durell said. "But if we sit here on our hands, we'll all be dead men by tomorrow night. Agosto will have to wipe us out."

"When is the Indian coming?"

"In a few minutes."

They waited in silence. Inocenza stood at the door of

the bunkhouse. O'Hara grumbled to himself in one of the bunks. His relief at learning that Durell had not come to revenge his grandmother had made the old man high, and he kept drinking heavily from his bottle, apparently to celebrate the ending of a lifelong nightmare.

Outside, the compound was filled with dark shadows. The wind that had moved in the swamp became stronger now, and the night whispered and crackled under the hot tropical stars. The Indian that Durell had knocked out earlier was securely gagged and lashed to one of the bunks. The main house was dark except for the perimeter lights where Agosto's patrols moved relentlessly. Durell studied the area from the doorway, then turned his attention to the other bungalows in the compound. There was a dim light among the Russians, another in the Chinese quarters. He did not know where the British, French, Yugoslav, and others were located, but he had already identified the last in the row, nearest the airstrip, as Atimboku's. A nagging worry and a sense of guilt tagged him. He had not seen or heard from Sally since their arrival. It could well be that Atimboku, win or lose in the bidding, would take advantage of the situation to eliminate his sister and consolidate his exclusive claim to rule the African state of Pakuru.

His worry intensified. The bungalow down there had been dark all night. Guards patrolled the airstrip beyond it, the hangar area, and the compound. Sooner or later someone would come here to relieve the guard he had knocked out. Agosto would be especially alert, sleepless, knowing that the others would be calculating their chances of getting away alive.

Mucujai did not show up.

Another ten minutes went by.

Wells moved silently beside him in the doorway. "He won't come, Cajun. These people won't fight each other, just to get even for the professor."

"They might," Durell said. "Mucujai has different loyalties from ours."

"Maybe we ought to try to take over, ourselves."

"We wouldn't have a chance."

"Maybe the British and the French—"

"They aren't doing anything."

"Sam, if they've figured out that Agosto plans to kill off all those who don't win the formula, on the one hand, and that the other copy will be published if any of us knock Agosto off—"

"It's a supposition, Willie. I just pulled it out of a hat, to confuse the bidding arrangements. But Agosto is not only the cruelest man in the business; he's also one of the craftiest and most unpredictable."

"But suppose *you* bid tomorrow and win the formula?"

"All the others privately hope to survive by winning that way, too. But could you take the formula and fly out of here and leave all the others to Agosto's firing squad?"

The black man's face went peculiarly blank. "Are you talking about a matter of conscience, Cajun?"

"I think so."

"That's something you're not supposed to have in our business. A conscience, I mean."

"Willie, would you leave Inocenza here to be among those who are massacred?"

"Uh. You notice that we get along, do you?"

"I noticed."

"And you want to get Sally safely away from Agosto, yourself, don't you?"

"I intend to."

"Then there is no use talking about getting out of here by ourselves, is there?"

Durell started to reply, then moved out another step from the doorway. There was movement in the shadows out there, running men, moving from darkness to darkness. The tropical night remained silent, but it was filled with unbearable electric tension, as if another storm was about to break. He heard the slap of naked feet running behind the bungalow and leaped to the corner as a man came around it from the left. There was no time to question or challenge the dark shadow. A weapon glinted, coming up, and Durell threw a fist into the enraged, frantic face, caught the other's rifle barrel, twisted it away and down. The man stumbled, lost his grip on the gun, and went spinning away. His big straw hat came off, cartwheeling into the darkness. Durell chopped and missed and chopped again. He heard a grunt of pain, the man's mouth opened to yell, and Durell hit him a last time. The Indian fell against the bungalow wall, his knees buckling, and then he slid downward on his shouders. Durell caught up the rifle, saw the man grope for a sidearm, and swung the rifle against the Indian's head. There was no more resistance. The man slid over on one side and lay still. As he picked up both the pistol and the rifle, he heard Willie Wells.

"All right, Cajun?"

"Fine. Slip out there and get his hat." His head throbbed and his pulse hammered in his bruised leg. Wells was a black shadow in the windy night. Durell said, "Take the pistol. Give Belmont the rifle."

"Good. Mucujai is here."

"I know."

The big Indian had a band of cartridge clips for the Uzi he carried and another pistol, which he gave to Inocenza. Wells moved next to the girl in a protective gesture. Mucujai said, "I have only twenty men so far, senhor. I only spoke to those I was sure of, so that none might warn the colonel. I do not know about the others."

"How many arms do you have?"

"We have given some to the Englishmen and to the Germans and to the African prince—"

"Hell," Durell said. "Which bungalow?"

Mucujai looked dismayed. "Did I do something wrong, senhor?"

"Not exactly. Go on up with your men to the house, but don't raise an alarm. Wait for me."

"*Sim,* senhor."

The big Indian faded away into the gloom. Wells said, "Coming, Cajun?"

"I have to stop Atimboku. He'll go to Agosto, if he can."

"And check on Sally?"

"Yes."

Durell moved at a swift trot toward the airstrip. He

heard a shot and an outbreak of yelling from near the hacienda, and at the same moment, a shadow rose up before him, gun in hand. No man knew friend from foe tonight. He yelled, "Mucujai!" but the unknown Indian snarled and fired. Durell squeezed off a triple burst from the rifle and sent the man fluttering backward. He redoubled his stride toward Atimboku's bunkhouse, although his bruises protested. Then he heard Sally scream and saw her slim figure from the doorway of the bungalow. Two shots were fired, smashing the night wide open.

"This way, Sally!" he called.

She hesitated, searching for him, and Atimboku lunged from the bunkhouse after her. Now shots sounded all over the compound and the main house, mixed with men's screams. The element of surprise in Mucujai's rebellion was lost. He swore and ran for Sally; but Atimboku caught her and flung her to the ground. The African heard him coming and snapped a thin strangling cord around his sister's neck.

"Hold it, Durell."

"Let her go."

"To hell with you. What's going on?"

"You should have figured it out. When Agosto killed Tovacheck, he put himself in a corner. He's going to have to execute all of us. Nobody left to kill him and force publication of the Zero Formula from wherever he hid his extra copy."

"I thought of that. But I'll get the formula. So don't try to stop me, or Sally gets—"

"Let her go," Durell said again.

The girl was on her knees, the strangling cord held tightly in Atimboku's grip. One jerk, and the knot would crush her larynx. Her golden eyes showed no fear. Her robe had been torn, and her long brown thigh showed taut muscles as she knelt, erect, like some sacrificial maiden at a pagan alter.

Atimboku grinned. "Drop your gun, Cajun."

Durell shot him through the left arm, and the bullet spun the tall African halfway around. The pull of the strangling cord took Sally backward off her knees. Durell yanked the cord loose. She began to cough, her hands at her throat. Atimboku tried to rise, but he was not the finely honed jungle animal Durell had known years ago. His reaction time was slow. Durell looked up and saw the surviving seven-foot warrior come charging out of the bunkhouse. He shot the man in the thigh, and he went down with a howl of dismay. Atimboku groaned and hugged his wounded arm.

"Get up, Sally," Durell said quietly.

She stood, shaking, and he touched her throat. Her voice quivered. "This time he was going to kill me, Sam."

"He always meant to kill you, Sally." Durell heard a sudden burst of renewed gunfire from the hacienda, took the girl's hand, and ran for the airstrip. The guards there were indecisive. There came a closer burst of automatic fire and two of the guards went down. The others at the hangar threw away their weapons and ran off. Belmont and Wells came running up.

"Take care of Sally for a moment," Durell said.

He ducked inside the open hangar doors. The place smelled of gasoline and machine oil. The Bell chopper looked like a giant, bubbled insect in the shadows. The Cessna was parked beside it. It took only seconds to check each plane and pull the ignition keys from the instrument panels. He pocketed them and called to the others.

"Willie. Belmont. Each of you take one of these fuel cans. Sally, you can carry one, too. Let's go."

He was afraid they had lost too much time already, but as they ran with their burdens across the compound, he saw that the fighting at the hacienda had hardly begun. There were confused challenges, a few desultory shots; but everyone had taken cover. The perimeter lights still blazed. But nothing visible moved near there now.

"The generator," Durell said. "Knock it out, Willie." He paused. "Take Inocenza with you."

"Sure thing."

They moved up toward the knoll, Sally close to his side. Wells vanished into the darkness, and a voice suddenly called from one of the last bungalows across the compound.

"Durell! Comrade Durell!"

He turned and saw Vodaniev and his men. "Yes?"

"What are you trying to do?" the Russian demanded.

"Starting a revolution," Durell said grimly. "Against Agosto. Want to join us?"

Vodaniev looked aghast. "A revolution, comrade?"

"Think about it," Durell said, and went on.

# 4

Mucujai was in a thicket of wild oleander, growing along a crumbled wall of what might once have been a formal garden attached to the hacienda. The Indian lowered his rifle as he recognized Durell. Mucujai looked grim. There was a bad gash across his broad cheek. He moved his head to indicate the lighted area around the big house.

"It is a fortress, senhor, with machine guns. My people in there cannot be approached. They fight for the colonel. They do not know that we, their brothers, are here. The colonel has told them we are foreigners, trying to trick them."

Durell pulled Sally down behind the crumbled stone wall. The generator plant was to the left. The house windows were all shuttered, but there were loopholes visible where rifles glinted. Mucujai's men had formed a loose circle around the knoll to seal off Agosto's escape, but the ring could be broken easily by a planned sortie that concentrated at one point of Mucujai's lines. Durell couldn't guess what Agosto was thinking. He would probably call for a parley soon, and try to turn the Indians against each other, offering something to them in lieu of the inevitable execution they might expect. Durell did not count on aid from the other bidders. They would wait for the outcome before acting. Vodaniev and Soo would follow their separate orders and watch each other as much as the struggle against Agosto. Each would be thinking of the Zero Formula. He wished he could guess what was hatching in Agosto's fertile brain. The man had made a mistake when he killed the professor, he knew it now, and he would plan a reply and an alternative to the present situation. He would try to turn the bidders against each other, of course—

The perimeter lights went out.

There was a sudden glow of fire from the shed that housed the diesel generator. Wells had succeeded in his task. The flames lit up the left side of the hacienda, and a sudden volley of shots came from that direction. But directly ahead, the walls of the big house were still in the shadows.

Durell stood up.

"Now, Mucujai. Sally, you stay here."

"No, Sam. I must go with you."

Her voice was adamant. He did not argue. He climbed the broken garden wall and dropped into tall weeds on the other side. Mucujai shouted in a shrill voice, and from all around them in the dark night the Indians arose and began to run toward the big house. Durell still carried his can of gasoline. Sally kept hers, too. Belmont came over the wall like a long, skinny cat.

"Which way, Sam?"

"The laboratory shed."

They ran to the right behind the screen of Indians. The darkness was filled with shots and screams. Sally panted under the cumbersome weight of her fuel can, but she did not abandon it. Broken masonry hampered them, and an abominable tangle of vines clutched at them and tripped them, then another wall. A machine gun stitched a bloody message into the fabric of the night. At the second wall, Durell paused. What remained of a high terrace loomed dimly before them. The stars were fading; the night was at its darkest now. Something slithered away in panic through the spiky undergrowth. An animal or a lizard, he thought. The clear area before them was exposed to windows in the right wing of the hacienda. Beyond the house he glimpsed the shed roof of the laboratory, but the night shadows made everything blurred and indistinct.

"Belmont?"

"Yes."

"I'll take your gasoline. Sally, this time you wait here with Belmont. I mean it. Both of you cover me."

She nodded agreement and he picked up her can of fuel, balancing it against his own, and left his rifle with Sally. There was a vague path that circled the house across the open area of the terrace. He was halfway across when the automatic rifle opened up on him from an upper window. He could see the muzzle flashes as the rifleman sought him out. Twigs snapped near him. He ran faster with his awkward burden of sloshing gasoline. Behind him, Belmont started firing in short, savage bursts at the gunman's window. Durell flung himself to the ground at the corner of the laboratory. The vague shape of a door showed in the plank wall. He left his two gasoline cans and tried the handle. It was locked. There were no windows. Behind him, Durell heard Belmont's gun again. He backed up a bit and hit the door with his shoulder. The planks proved to be flimsy and rotten. The lock burst apart. He went back for the fuel cans and stepped through the broken doorway.

Someone moved in behind him, blocking his escape.

"Sam?"

It was Willie Wells and Inocenza. Light from a sudden burst of flames in the generator building outlined the couple against the night.

Durell said, "Let's get to work."

"Don't we look for any data we could take home with us?" Wells asked.

"No."

"I don't get it."

"We burn everything. Here and now."

"Sam, we're supposed to get the formula."

"It wouldn't be here. Do you want *anybody* to get it, Willie?"

"Not the Russians or the Chinese, that's for sure."

"Then start in with the gasoline."

There was a smell of chemicals, a glint of glass and stainless steel laboratory equipment, the shape of a compressor, a row of small steel tanks stacked up like a pile of hundred-pound aerial bombs. Benches, tables littered with

equipment, a row of filing cabinets along the house wall.
For a moment, he was tempted to search. A double door
was set in the interior house wall. He tested the latch carefully. It was not locked. He did not open it yet. The sharp
smell of splashing gasoline filled the black air. Inocenza
stayed very close to Wells, helping him. Suddenly there
was firing from just outside the laboratory, on the terrace
they had crossed. Men yelled. Someone paused in the broken outer door of the lab and Wells raised his gun, only to
be halted by a gesture from Durell. The man looked in,
did not see them in the interior gloom, and moved on. Inocenza let out a small sigh.

"We are trapped in here?"

"Willie, use your matches. We'll go on into the house.
The stone wall will keep the flames from us."

Wells said, "Into the lion's den?"

"Agosto is no lion."

He opened the double-leafed door and drew Inocenza
through. She fell against him, her body pliant and yielding,
but she quickly pulled away and looked back at Wells.
Willie's match was a small bomb flare in the darkness. The
gasoline burst into flames with a tremendous *whoosh!* and
then a flat, explosive sound, as Willie jumped back into
the main house. They were in a wide, square room filled
with rubbish and cobwebs; it might once have been a
salon or a library. In the great burst of red light, Durell
saw that the room was empty. The heat struck them like a
giant slap in the face. They retreated across the dusty
room, the roar of the flames covering their quick steps.
The opposite doors led into a narrow hall, where a few
fallen timbers lay at odd angles from the collapsed ceiling.
They climbed quickly through and over the obstructions.
This wing of the house had never been reconstructed.
Durell heard feet running overhead, a spatter of shots. A
door at the end of the corridor was flung open and two figures tumbled through. Again Durell checked Willie's automatic move with his gun. It was Belmont and Sally, di-
sheveled and panting. A long scratch bled on Belmont'
cheek. Sally looked unharmed.

"Figured you'd be nearby." Belmont drew a deep

breath and Sally leaned against the wall to rest. Belmont's eyes gleamed red in the glow of the fire behind them. "Mucujai's going to get his ass shot off. Tried a frontal attack over there." He flipped a hand to the right. "Got beaten back."

"Let's find Agosto," Durell said.

"Cajun, he's for me. Remember that."

A small stairway led them up to the next level. This wing had once been used to house domestic servants. Durell paused at the top of the narrow steps. A door here leaned askew on broken hinges. The light from the lab fire was cut off up here. Durell squeezed through the broken doorway and the others followed. No one was in sight. The hall ran the length of the wing. About thirty feet onward was an intersecting corridor leading to the central section of the hacienda. The floor creaked dangerously underfoot. There was an odor of decay, of many years of emptiness, mingled with dust and mold that splotched the walls like cancerous growths. There were shouts and more running feet from below now, as Agosto's men fought the laboratory fire. An Indian ducked from the intersecting corridor, saw them, opened his mouth to yell a warning. Durell hit him and the man fell toward Belmont, who hit him again. They went on into the main upper corridor.

Apparently most of Agosto's men were below now. There was a series of empty rooms along one side of the hallway, but the windows had been abandoned as firing posts. Durell moved swiftly ahead through the dimness. Smoke curled after them, close on their heels. He felt a growing sense of unease. Something was wrong. If he missed Agosto, if the man escaped somehow, unpredictably, he might team up with the Russians or Mr. Soo. Anything could happen, then. Agosto might make a sortie for the airstrip and the planes there. It was one reason Durell had removed the ignition keys from the Cessna and the Bell chopper.

He passed the radio room, stopped, went back.

In the dim red light, he saw that someone had effectively smashed the transmitting equipment. Agosto, probably.

It didn't matter now, with the generator knocked out and no power available. He turned back. Belmont was gone.

"Where is he?"

Sally said, "He ran on ahead."

"He wants Agosto real bad," Wells added. His face gleamed with sweat. "Sam, I think Agosto outsmarted us."

"We'll try the theater," Durell decided.

Another flight of stairs took them down into gloom and dust. The smoke was thicker here. The theater doors were to the right. Durell felt a tight apprehension. He heard the distant shouts of Agosto's men fighting the fire, but there were no more gunshots. Mucujai had been beaten off. He smelled dust, heat, the slow decomposition of decades. He stepped through the wide doors.

It was too late.

Belmont was on the stage. He looked like a giant insect caught up in a tight bag of spider webs. The single oil lamp that served as a footlight shone up at his white face, his glaring eyes. He had been caught in a spring-snare hidden on the stage, tripped by his unwary footstep. Covered by a piece of loose canvas, with innocent-looking lines leading back, had been a net that had lifted him high in the bag when weights for hoisting scenery had been tripped. The weights still swung like slow pendulums. The trap had been a device contrived by Agosto for unwelcome intruders. Belmont hung in the bag, an arm and leg projecting, the rest of him trapped like a bug in a cocoon, and Durell wasn't sure if he was alive or dead.

"Belmont?" he called softly.

Too late, he knew that he had been drawn into Agosto's trap, too.

# Chapter Thirteen

THE little theater seemed empty, except for Belmont's enmeshed figure on the stage. Durell knew it was not. There was no way to keep Wells and Sally and Inocenza from moving in behind him. Inocenza made a small moaning sound when she saw Belmont's helpless figure. Sally drew close to Durell. He put a hand out to ward her away from him, to give him room to move. Wells moved to the opposite wall beside the door. For a moment, then, no one moved. The oil lamp cast strange shadows on the former delicacy of the private little theater. A few glints of gold still shone on the painted curlicues of the boxes above. All the seats were empty. The silence in here rang with danger.

"Belmont?" Durell called softly. "Agosto?"

Someone laughed. It was a harsh, incongruous sound, followed by a stumble, a curse, another belch of laughter. Durell could not miss the identity of that voice.

"O'Hara!"

The fat old man came on stage warily, peering here and there. He clutched his inevitable bottle in a wavering paw. He stumbled again, glared at Belmont, who hadn't moved in his truss of nets, and squinted out from under his shaggy brows, through the light of the flickering oil lantern. Footsteps padded in the main hall beyond the theater entrance.

"That you, Samuel?"

"Yes."

"He's got you."

"I know."

O'Hara grinned wickedly and poked at the net that held Belmont. "Got your man here, too!"

"Is Belmont dead?"

"Maybe."

"Where is Agosto?"

"Coming."

Inocenza began to swear to herself in Tupamara dialect. Behind them, Durell heard more footsteps and saw other guards move in through the side doors of the theater and felt a gun probe at his back. They were enclosed in as effective a net as was Belmont, on the stage. The gun muzzle in his back became urgent. He moved forward down the aisle to where the bidders had conducted the auction last night.

*"Capitão!"* Inocenza called. "Have you betrayed us?"

"No, child. He just caught me." O'Hara sweated suddenly. "Durell was right. He's goin' to kill us all."

"Come down here, O'Hara," Durell said.

The old man came down the side steps of the stage, holding his dirty white pants up around his belly. At the same moment, Agosto appeared on the stage like a player on cue.

He wore a neat, clean bush jacket with a holstered pistol at his belt. The leather was shiny and polished. His brown pleasant face and black eyes smiled. He might have been the long-dead Don Federico, coming to welcome his elegant rubber-baron guests. It was difficult to believe that behind his gentle, engaging smile, there existed a brain as cold as the outer fringes of hell.

"Gentlemen!"

His armed guards formed a circle around Durell's party, covering them with enough guns, Durell thought, to contain a military company. None of the Indians, presumably, belonged to Mucujai's rebellious party. A thin curl of smoke entered the theater by way of the back stage. Agosto glanced at the gray tendril, but only smiled again.

"Gentlemen, you see how foolish you have been. You have only done my work for me. Obviously, as I promised, I meant to put this place to the torch, myself. Durell, have you your letter of credit?"

"Yes."

"You were searched. It was not found. Why did you not bid for the formula last night?"

"I'm not buying," Durell said.

"You thought you could steal it by force?"

"I thought I could destroy it."

"Ah, yes. But you have failed, eh?"

"Not yet."

"The Indians you managed to disaffect are defeated. These here are loyal to me alone. As is so often the case among people in your profession, you see that the Russians, the Chinese, all the others, they have stayed clear of your abortive attempt to destroy me."

"It's not over yet," Durell said.

"You still try to bluff me? I will have your letter of credit now. Please. Do not resist. Your life is not important to me."

"The amount is not yet filled out," Durell said.

"I will not be greedy. Let us make it a round hundred million," Agosto smiled.

"And the formula?"

"I have it here."

More smoke surged in from behind the stage. One of the Indians coughed nervously. The sound of crackling flames touched them. Durell looked at Belmont's figure, hanging in the net onstage, snarled in the lines. The stage weights that had hoisted the trap had stopped their gentle swinging. Belmont's eyes still glared lifelessly at them from amid the shrouds; thick blood oozed from a head wound and covered the left side of his face; but Durell thought there had been a slight change in the man's position. One arm projecting from the bagged web was a bit lower now. Agosto never bothered to look at his captive, who hung there like a giant netted fish taken from the Amazon.

Agosto reached in one of the pockets of his bush jacket and held aloft a shining, stainless steel capsule. Then he carefully unscrewed the two halves of the four-inch container and took from it a small roll of paper.

"The Zero Formula, Senhor Durell. The complete description of the device and how it functions. The Zero Formula, for which you and the others, who are foolish not to be here at this moment, traveled so far to buy."

Agosto was not smiling now. "It is yours. Yours, for your nation exclusively, as long as you insure my life."

"I'm not buying," Durell said again.

Sally drew in a long, sighing breath. Wells moved closer to Inocenza. It was doubtful, Durell thought, if the guards who surrounded them with their palisade of weapons knew what was going on. He looked at Belmont again, in the net above the stage, but nothing had changed.

More smoke hazed the air in the theater. Some of the Indians stirred restlessly. The pop and crackle of the fire was distinct now as the flames roared closer.

O'Hara whispered hoarsely, "For God's sake, Durell, you can't hold out against him. He's got all the aces."

"Not quite."

Agosto spoke from the height of the stage. "You play for time, Senhor Durell? But time has run out for both of us, for you and for me. I offer you the exclusive rights to the formula. It is what you came for. It is what your orders expressly bid you to obtain. It is yours, senhor, if you have your letter of credit, as you say."

Agosto called one of the Indians forward and spoke in a rapid spate of Tupamara dialect. He then switched back to English, and there was a venom in his voice. "My man will strip you, Durell, and he will not do it gently. I want your letter of credit now, signed, sealed and delivered."

"How can I trust you?" Durell asked.

"Do you have a choice? I have canceled the auction, since your competitors stay in their bungalows and do not appear. It is your good fortune, senhor. When you produce the credits, I hand you the formula and dismiss the Indians. You must leave at once, however. A plane will be provided to fly you to Paramaguito. From there, other transportation will be made available."

"And you will stay here with the others?"

"I will stay, but I shall be alone."

"Then you are condemning my competitors to death. You ask me to be a party to a massacre."

"It was you who forced the issue, who made them aware of the inevitable end to this little game of mine. You caused them to know that I had to kill everyone here, except for you and me." Agosto's voice was virulent now. "You showed them that for my own safety, to prevent publication of the second copy if I were killed, they would have to die." The haze in the little theater was growing stronger, acrid and thick. "Come. I have been more than courteous to you."

Durell saw Sally's eyes on him. They held a plea in their golden depths he could not define. He shrugged and slipped off his wide belt, unsnapped the buckle, and tugged. The outer seams of the stitched leather had already been opened and searched. But inside, there was another slot that had been overlooked, which came open when the buckle was detached. He thrust a finger inside and took out the folded letter of credit that Kevin Kendall had given to him in Geneva.

"Here it is."

"Now. Very good. You will fill out the sum of one hundred million dollars, which I am sure has been deposited in this account, eh? And you will sign it."

Agosto's flat-faced Indian guard produced a ball-point pen. Something made a sudden cracking sound in the domed ceiling overhead. A long tongue of angry flame licked down from above. The Indians murmured. Durell did not look up. He filled in the formal letter of credit and signed it.

Agosto looked pleased. "You are a sensible and practical man, Senhor Durell."

"But you are not," Durell said.

The ceiling began to fall in.

## 2

The Indians shouted and drew back in alarm from the shower of falling, burning timbers. At the same moment, there was a swift squirming in the net suspended above the stage behind Agosto. Belmont was very much alive. With his loose hand that projected from the web, he reached in and pulled a flashing knife from a strap attached to his calf. The net came apart in long, looping strands, releasing him. He came down on Agosto's back like a long, skinny spider pouncing from the center of its web.

A flaming timber fell among the Indians, who yelled and screamed as the heavy timber smashed one man's head and pinned two others under its massive weight. Durell pushed Sally down between the seats and jumped for the stage. The guards were too terrified by the collapsing ceiling to stop him. He heard a single shot from Agosto's gun. It was a confused struggle under the tangled pieces of netting that had been Belmont's prison. Willie Wells jumped to the stage beside him, a gun in his hand taken from one of the guards. Durell coughed in the thick gush of smoke that filled the theater. A sudden wall of heat encompassed him, and he held his breath while he grabbed for Agosto's hand through ropes of the net. Agosto held his gun at Belmont's head. Durell chopped at the neck of Agosto's neck with all his strength. He heard the vertebrae snap. Stainless steel flickered in Agosto's fingers. He grabbed for the small cylinder, caught it, wrenched it free. Then he jumped clear himself, pulled at Agosto's arm, turning the gun away from Belmont's face. But there was no resistance, suddenly. The man's fingers were limp.

"Belmont?"

"Yo, Cajun." It was a harsh whisper. "He shot me in the gut. It's real bad."

"Agosto?"

"You broke his neck."

Agosto had no answer to make. Belmont's knife was stuck into the man's ribs up to the hilt. Agosto's suave face was already swollen and darkening; the black eyes stared, the white teeth gleamed from under the small, neat moustache.

"Is he dead yet?" Belmont gasped.

"Yes."

"You got the formula?"

"Yes."

Belmont started to cough, grinned up at Durell in the red glare of the burning theater, then coughed again as blood suddenly gushed from his open mouth. Durell struggled to pull him out of the net, but Belmont's eyes were fixed, staring in sightless triumph.

"Cajun," Wells said sharply. "Belmont is gone."

Durell pocketed the stainless steel cylinder that contained the Zero Formula. "Let's get out of here."

One entire wall of the theater was ablaze now. The heat struck at them furiously. The Indian guards—those who had survived the collapse of the ceiling—had fled. Durell paused and looked at the fire. All of the others had scrambled up to the relative safety of the stage.

"Sam!" Willie called imperatively.

"In a moment."

Durell unscrewed the metal cylinder, and took out the small roll of paper inside. It was covered with esoteric biological engineering symbols which meant very little to him. He looked at it for a moment, then added the letter of credit he had signed, and crumpled both papers in a tightly wadded ball. With a single gesture, he flung both the formula and the money into the fire. In an instant, the papers burst into flames and turned into a black, twisted lump of ash.

"Let's go," he said.

# Chapter Fourteen

THEY took the Cessna, flying from the airstrip into a hot, bright dawn. Willie Wells was the pilot. He circled the old rubber plantation once, and they looked down on the smoking shell of the hacienda, the bunkhouses on the compound, the small Indian settlement on the banks of the river tributary. The clearing looked small and defenseless in the surrounding sea of wild, impacable jungle and swamp. The men they had left behind, Vladim Vodaniev and Mr. Soo and the others, were small ants milling about in angry puzzlement amid the wreckage.

"Do we maroon them all there?" Wells asked.

"No." Durell used the Cessna's radio to transmit to Paramaguito. The girl he had alerted there, Connie Drew, was awake and clever, on the job. He had a brief image of her on the docks, with her birdcages of kiskadees and the harpy eagle. She monitored his call, returned an acknowledgement. He thumbed the microphone button again. "We'll be landing in about an hour. After we leave for Belém, you can wait twenty-four hours and then tell the police there are some foreigners stranded at Don Federico's. They'll get around to pulling out the others."

"You want a head start, is that it?" Connie asked.

"I don't have anything for them to chase me for, but they may not know that," Durell acknowledged.

It was crowded in the Cessna, with O'Hara in the rear seat, Sally and Inocenza behind Wells and Durell. The sun came up in a burst of tropical glory, spreading light like hot melted butter over the forests and the river. It seemed only a few moments before they were over São Felice and heading downriver for Paramaguito and the Amazon.

On the last leg, Wells spoke, leaning forward to squint

into the glare of the sun. "Cajun, what will you tell Mr. Kendall and Mr. Carboyd?"

"I'll tell them the truth," Durell said.

"They won't buy it, Sam."

Durell smiled. "Agosto has contaminated you, Willie. Eventually, the formula will be published, when Agosto's death is known to his agent who has the other copy."

"You paid a high price for your gesture, Sam."

"Yes. So did Andy Weyer. And Belmont."

Wells said, "I'd like to stay in Paramaguito for a bit, Sam. Just a couple of days. A week, if you can possibly stretch it."

"All right."

"You see, Inocenza and I—"

"You don't have to explain."

When they landed at the river junction, Connie Drew was at the airport, squatting in the shade, barefooted, wearing her ragged denims. She had her cages of brightly colored birds beside her and she tried to sell them to incoming tourists and road engineers.

"Hooey," she said. "You all look beat."

"We are."

"I fixed up some rooms for all of you at the Hotel *O Rei Felipe.* Is that okay?"

"I want to go right on to Belém," Durell said.

The girl sighed and looked at him. "That figures. Work is your gig, right? You don't know how to relax and enjoy nature, do you? Natural things swing, you know? You owe me two hundred, too. My Indian kids need the bread."

"I'll send it upriver from Belém."

She looked at Willie Wells. "Can I trust him?"

"All the way," Wells said.

A special, private jet bearing a corporate engineering company insigne waited for them in the hot, dusty sunlight. O'Hara had gone into the airport bar and was drinking beer as if he might never get the chance again. Durell went through the ramshackle waiting room and came up to the bar beside the fat old man. O'Hara felt his presence, but did not turn around. There were electric fans and open shutter windows, Bahamian style, in the bar. Some road

engineers were arguing at the end of the bar, and a pretty
Brazilian stewardess was having a Coke with the pilot of
the regular commercial flight that had just come in.

"Now you chop my head off, huh?" O'Hara muttered.

"No."

"I want to tell you something, Samuel—"

"I think I know it already, *Capitão*."

"I loved your grandma, sonny. What I did back in those
days was real bad, really wrong. When she wouldn't play
my game, I offered to send her back to your grandpa Jonathan. She was ashamed and afraid to go back. I tried to
talk her into leavin' me. It wasn't easy. I wanted her like I
never wanted any other woman, before or after. I still
want her. But then she got sick with the fever, as soon as
we got here, and she died. Like she wanted to die, I reckon. I can't ever pay it back."

Durell ordered beer from the bartender. The stewardess
had looked over at him several times. Her slightly slanted
eyes were speculative. Through the window, he saw Sally
talking to Connie Drew.

O'Hara said heavily, "I'm going to miss the *Duos Irmãos*. You burned her up. I've got nothin' left at the end
of my life. Not even Inocenza."

"I'll see to it that my 'company' finances a new riverboat for you."

"Won't ever be the same."

"Nothing is ever the same," Durell said.

"You going to tell your grandpappy about me?"

"Yes, when I get home."

"I still don't know what all you fellers were up to."

"I hope you never know, *Capitão*."

He started to put his hand on the old man's shoulder,
changed his mind, and walked out of the bar, into the sunlight where Sally waited for him.

## 2

She was long and cool, all liquid gold, sleeping beside
him. The sheets were crisp and new. The hotel room in the

*Gran Prao Excelsior* was air-conditioned, the shutters closed, the sign on the corridor door requested no disturbance. They had made love, slept for twelve hours, ordered dinner sent up, served by solicitous waiters, and then they went back to bed again. The hacienda of Don Federico was a fading nightmare, thirty-six hours behind them.

Durell slid out of the big bed without waking her. Sally's hair lay in an ebony cascade over the white pillows. She lay with one knee drawn up, her hip and thigh long and sensual under the pale flowered coverlet. Dimly, the sound of traffic came from Belém's boulevards, the Praca da Republica. When he moved the draperies a bit, he was surprised to see it was night again, and the neon and electric lights of Belém's aggressive advertising signs made gaudy splashes against the hot, tropical sky. The city was all white stone and red tiled roofs, incongruously comingled with the ubiquitous steel and glass business towers spread all around the world.

He thought of taking Sally to the Goeldi Museum, the Bosque, the docks at the Ver o Peso market. He watched a jet roar in from the south, from Rio, probably a *Verig Cruzeiro* plane. From the height of the hotel-room window, he saw an old wood-burning river steamer of the ENASA lines, chuffing against the current toward Manaus on its bimonthly five-day trip. He closed the curtain and looked back at the bed.

Sally was awake.

She was shivering. Her eyes were frightened.

"Sam?"

"It's all right."

"I had a nightmare."

"I know."

"Do I talk in my sleep?"

"A little. It was mostly in Banda dialect. I didn't get all of it. You're still afraid of your brother, Prince Tim, is that it?"

"Should we have looked for him before we left, Sam?"

"He wanted to kill you, Sally."

"Atimboku is still my brother."

He remembered the bittersweet manner in which they

had made love, the desperation of her passion, a clinging to what could never be again.

"I think Prince Atimboku Mari Mak Mujilikaka is dead," he said. "He died of his own greed, his lust for power. Being the ruler of Pakuru in Africa killed him."

"Yes," Sally whispered. Her golden eyes mourned. "But he could have been—he could have done so much—"

"But he didn't."

"And that means that I—according to our laws, Sam—I have to take his place."

He smiled gently. "The Queen Elephant."

"What a horrible title."

"Your mother carried it proudly."

"I thought I wanted to rule my country. I'm not so sure now, Sam. I wish I didn't have to go back."

"You must."

Her golden eyes sorrowed. "I'll never be able to be myself again, if I do. My true self. I'll never be able to see you except formally, as a ruling queen, even if you do ever return to Pakuru one day."

"Yes."

The telephone rang.

He had been expecting it.

He said, "I'll have to leave you for a short time. Only an hour or two. You'll be hearing from your own consulate in the morning. We have until then."

The phone kept ringing.

He crossed the darkened room and picked it up.

"Yes, Mr. Carboyd," he said. "This is Durell."

## 3

Kevin Kendall and Homer Carboyd had taken an executive suite on the top floor of the hotel. A small sign on the door had the insigne of a mineral exploration company —the same insigne which had been on the private jet that had flown them from Paramaguito. It was one of many K Section subsidiary covers. From the wide glass windows, he could see all the lights of the City of Our Lady of Bethlehem, spangling the dark night. Both men wore their usual dark suits, white shirts, dark neckties. Kevin Kendall looked slender and dapper, his silver hair neatly groomed, a small sad smile on his lips. Homer Carboyd had the same bulldog expression of distaste that he had displayed back in Prince John, Maryland.

"You didn't really do it," Carboyd rumbled.

"Yes, sir. I did."

"You destroyed the formula?"

"Yes, sir."

"And the letter of credit?"

"Yes."

"Will you, for sweet Jesus' sake, tell me *why?*" Carboyd exploded.

"One moment, Homer." Kendall spoke in his mild Boston accent. "There were certain terms and conditions Durell put forth when he accepted the job—"

"You stay out of this, Kevin. I represent Sugar Cube. The President himself. We were prepared to pay plenty for the Zero Formula. You had practically unlimited funds, Durell. We could have used the formula exclusively, for some political leverage—"

"I didn't promise to bring it back for that purpose," Durell reminded him.

"You committed treason, goddam it! You destroyed a highly classified government property—"

"It was never an American property. I never bid on it. I never really bought it. I just destroyed it."

Homer Carboyd made a snorting noise through his flared, angry nostrils. His pale eyes glared at Durell's tall, quiet figure. "You're nitpicking. You had it in your hands, your report says. You lost two good men getting there. Your associate, Mr. Wells, admits you had it in your possession."

"And no chance of getting away alive with it, if the other bidders knew of it," Durell said. "In any case, I took on the job with specific qualifications. I didn't trust you, Mr. Carboyd, to abide by those qualifications. You have condemned yourself just now by suggesting you had ideas for using the formula as a weapon for terror, blackmail, perhaps as the red button to destroy the world's ecology and mankind with it. I used my own judgment. I destroyed the thing."

Kevin Kendall said mildly, "But you say it will be published, eventually, in any case."

"Maybe. We don't know how many lies the man we knew as Agosto told us, or pretended to have arranged. I think he was bluffing. I think he had only the one copy I saw. There may be no other in existence, anywhere in the world."

"But he said there was."

"We may find out, someday. But then, everyone will have it, if that's the case. The balance will remain. No one nation can threaten the rest of the world with it."

Kendall said, "You wanted it that way?"

"Yes."

"But suppose the other copy—if it exists—falls into private hands, is sold to our enemies and rivals. Then everything you did becomes useless, a real loss to our country."

"Agosto wouldn't arrange it that way," Durell said quietly. "He would want his revenge, even from the grave. He said he had arranged it so that this alleged copy would be published after a specific time passed that meant he was dead. He wouldn't want to let all the fruits of his planning and scheming to go to anyone else. No, Mr. Kendall. No, Mr. Carboyd. You can forget about the Zero Formula becoming the exclusive property of any one nation."

Carboyd took out one of his Havana cigars and chewed on it angrily. "I'll see to it that there is a complete investigation of your behavior, Durell. By God, I could have you crucified!"

Kevin Kendall said, "That would not be wise, Homer."

"No? But he destroyed the formula, he—"

"Sam, do you think you accomplished anything?"

Durell said, very quietly, "Yes. We've removed one more weapon of terror from the world."

Homer Carboyd chewed savagely on his cigar and paced the room for a moment. It seemed as if Durell's quiet words hung tangibly in the hotel room.

Kevin Kendall finally said, "Sam, have you had a doctor look at you?"

"Yes. I'm all right."

"You need some sleep. We'll see you in D.C. soon enough, I expect."

"Yes, sir. I have to see about Andy Weyer's grave. And I'll have to set up a new Central here in Belém."

"Of course."

Durell said, "Mr. Carboyd?"

The big man waved a hand in dismissal. "Go on. Do as Kevin says. You do look a bit tired."

## 4

He went back to the suite that Sally shared with him. There was a living room, a tiled bath, and two separate bedrooms. The bed where he had left Sally was empty. He looked for her in the shadows at the window and on the small balcony that overlooked the city. She was not there. The night air outside was warm and tranquil. Overhead, the equatorial stars blazed solemnly in a sky of velvet. Even at this height, he could smell the sweet-scented trees that lined Belém's streets. He thought of the blossoms that gave off their fragrance down there and remembered the bleak sterility of George's Fields. It would not happen again.

He turned back inside, into the dark refrigerated air of the hotel rooms. Her bedroom door was closed. He tried the handle. It was locked.

"Sally?"

He felt an odd relief when he heard her reply and knew she was there. The past few days had made him jumpy.

"Go away, Sam," she said.

"Sally, tomorrow it will all be over. Tomorrow you will fly back to Africa and I'll go back to Washington."

"Yes."

"Open the door, Sally."

There was a long silence. The hotel management had thoughtfully provided him with a bottle of bourbon and a small box of thin Brazilian cigars. His body ached with a score of bruises, contusions, lacerations. He looked at the new Seiko watch he had bought this afternoon. Six hours to dawn. He would have to go to Bayou Peche Rouge, in Louisiana, to see his grandfather and tell him about Clarissa. It would end a nightmare that had lasted most of a lifetime for that old man, too. Later, he would go to Prince John, when Deirdre was there, and they would enjoy the peace and beauty of that old house, with the pink brick and the Chesapeake; he would take her sailing on the Bay and show her George's Fields. But that was for much later. He took a long drink of the bourbon and it hit his stomach like acid. The cigar tasted raw. He waited, watching the stars.

After a time he heard her door open.

"Sam?"

She stood there, naked, seeming defenseless.

"Salduva of Pakuru, go back to bed. Try to sleep. You're right, it's all over."

"I'm still Sally, until tomorrow. What did those men say to you, Sam? Are you in trouble for what you did?"

"Nothing too important. Nothing they won't have to forget soon."

"In my country, I would give you great honors and many medals. Will they punish you in any way?"

"I don't think so."

She came to the chair in which he sat and leaned over him and kissed him. Her ripe breasts were touched by the dim starlight that came in from the balcony windows. Liquid silver traced the graceful outlines of her hip and thigh.

"Please, Sam. I'm sorry. It hasn't been easy for me, either. I don't want to face tomorrow. I keep thinking of Atimboku, my brother. How he meant to kill me. But I don't know if he's alive or dead. I thought it might be best to end it between us, when you went to see those men from your government. Foolish me. For tonight, I'm still a foolish girl. Still your Sally. Time enough tomorrow to consider being the ruler of my country."

"True," Durell said.

"Come back to bed with me, Sam. For tonight."

He thought of Agosto and the formula. He hoped he had judged it correctly. He hoped Agosto had been lying; that the formula did not exist any more.

He thought of O'Hara and his grandfather.

He thought of Deirdre and the house on the Chesapeake Bay and the skipjack and the blossoms of spring.

More than the warm feminine fragrance of Sally made him stand up. It was here. It was now.

He took her hand and walked with her to the bedroom.

Tomorrow was another day. Tonight belonged to them.

# BIG NEW BESTSELLERS
# FROM FAWCETT GOLD MEDAL